Eternal Diet

Wendy Wilson

Copyright © 2019. All rights reserved.

This is a work of fiction. Names, characters, places, and incidents either are the product of the author's imagination or are used fictitiously. Any resemblance to actual persons, living or dead, events, or locales is entirely coincidental.

Disclaimer: Neither Chell Reads Publishing, or our authors will be responsible for repercussions to anyone who utilizes the subject of this book for illegal, immoral or unethical use.

This is a work of fiction. The views expressed herein do not necessarily reflect that of the publisher.

This book or part thereof may not be reproduced in any form, stored in a retrieval system, or transmitted in any form by any means-electronic, mechanical, photocopy, recording or otherwise-without prior written consent of the publisher, except as provided by United States of America copyright law.

Published by Chell Reads Publishing

ISBN:
Cover by Donna Cook
Second Edition Edits by Michelle Morrow www.chellreads.com

Contents

Chapter One	1
Chapter Two	15
Chapter Three	24
Chapter Four	29
Chapter Five	42
Chapter Six	53
Part Two	60
Chapter Seven	61
Chapter Eight	70
Chapter Nine	75
Chapter Ten	83
Chapter Eleven	91
Chapter Twelve	100
Chapter Thirteen	107
Chapter Fourteen	114
Chapter Fifteen	122
Chapter Sixteen	126
Chapter Seventeen	138
Chapter Eighteen	143
Chapter Nineteen	150
Chapter Twenty	153
Chapter Twenty-One	163
Chapter Twenty-Two	168

Chapter Twenty-Three	176
Chapter Twenty-Four	181
Chapter Twenty-Five	188
Chapter Twenty-Six	197
Chapter Twenty-Seven	213
Chapter Twenty-Eight	229
Chapter Twenty-Nine	250
Chapter Thirty	258
Chapter Thirty -One	268
Chapter Thirty -Two	281
Chapter Thirty -Three	288
Chapter Thirty -Four	299
Chapter Thirty-Five	304
Chapter Thirty-Six	307
Author Wendy Wilson	313

Chapter One

Gwendolyn J'sarajen, Gwen for short, wrung the washcloth out in the cold water and dragged it along her neck and around her sizable breast, sighing. Lifting one with her free hand, she wiped underneath and let it fall. She repeated with her other breast and continued down the contours of her overlapping belly rolls and down to the parting of her thighs.

She wasn't very tall, and her fat was centered mostly around her belly. People had told her; people who would know, she had pretty legs, so she tried to show them off every chance she got. Which, in the heat of New Orleans was often.

Her hair when she first moved to New Orleans was shoulder length. Long and thin, it was the only thing about her that *was* long and thin. But in this humidity, it just lay there. If she put it up into a ponytail, she had to twist the rubber band several times to keep it from slipping off. Finally, she went to a hairdresser and told the stylist to "cut it off, cut it all off." Now when she dealt with the sweat at least, her scalp was cooler. And, as she looked in the mirror, she grinned. 'I kinda rock the pixie look!'

Eternal Diet *Wendy Wilson*

Her mirror wasn't a full-length mirror, which was just as well. She didn't need to be reminded every single day she looked like an apple on toothpicks. The little mirror she had hanging above the table relayed more than enough information.

She continued to rinse and drag the now warm but still wet cloth around her body. A small fan on the dresser blew enough air to fool her body into believing it was cool. She so hated the heat and humidity that caused moisture to cling to crevices. Heat rash in New Orleans never seemed to go away, and bras and panties aggravated the condition resulting in some serious prickly heat.

Why did I move here? Wasn't Seattle a more comfortable climate? But she made New Orleans sound sooo much more promising. And frankly, sparkly doesn't suit me. Noooo, I had to go all romantic and pick the armpit of the nation because... Well, because, truthfully, it was the better location to follow my plan. All right, my OBSESSION.

At first, it had been a lot of fun; visiting all those wonderful restaurants and nightclubs; hanging out on corners with a large drink listening to the street musicians play all while the cops walked on by. Gwen had quickly hidden her beer behind her back the first time a cop passed her. "Hey girl, you don't have to hide your beer in Nawlins!" said a dark girl in dreads, "the cops are cool with it."

Gwen had gotten used to it quickly indeed. Especially the visiting the restaurant part. Gumbo and jambalaya and freshly caught seafood prepared by the chefs who knew how to do Cajun. She licked her lips for the memory. But little by little her savings grew smaller while she herself, grew larger and the visits to all the fancy restaurants had to be cut in favor of staying in and eating what she could cook on a single burner hot plate. And the favorite of many Americans; fast food, cheap and easy to get.

A flip of her wrist and the washcloth was hanging from a hook in the wall. Gwen walked around her tiny room, four steps from the door to the wall and five steps from the window to the bed. In between was a small dresser with a mirror and the fan and a wooden chair where a puppy had done some artful carving. Her few possessions remained packed in her suitcase. Except for her laptop; that was on the bed, always plugged in ready to record what she found.

McDonald's wrappers and cups laid strewn on the floor along with Styrofoam containers from walk-up soup vendors. A few dried fries with dabs of ketchup and the remains of a poorly cooked hamburger had almost made it to the garbage pail. A

Eternal Diet   *Wendy Wilson*

half-wrapped Twinkie sat on the windowsill. Without conscious thought, she unwrapped it and stared into the mist. *Maybe tonight.* The Twinkie went down in two bites and brushing the crumbs from her chest she turned and looked at the walls. Her obsession. Pasted on every blank space hung photos of pale, black-clad wraiths with colorless faces. Most cut from magazines advertising the latest vampire movie or book but some, and these fueled her search, were photos she had taken herself. And while the number of those was small, they were real. They showed the same image in each one; a tall rock star figure clad in black hurrying away from a scene invariably later described by the police as "incredibly neat considering how much blood the victim lost."

    The search for that elusive figure was what had driven her to quit her Winchester, Virginia existence and move to New Orleans, the new mecca of the modern-day Vampire and she was getting close. She had one video she was particularly proud of. It showed a dark alley and what she had seen one night. It had excited and frightened her so badly, she'd spent the following night in her room, afraid what she had captured had been real. She wasn't getting anywhere sitting in her room. Tonight, she would go out, damn the torpedoes, full speed ahead!

Eternal Diet *Wendy Wilson*

Fifteen minutes later, Gwen hurried down the staircase as a petulant voice called from the side room. "What are you doin' goin' out so late? It ain't safe for a girl here at night. Don't you read the papers? There's been stories of girls being kidnapped." Yeah, like some guy is gonna wanna rape me. "Ms. LaBeauf, it isn't all that late. I promise to be back soon." "And make sure you lock the door, missy. Last night the bolt wasn't thrown. No telling who coulda walked in." *I did make sure to set the deadbolt. Ah well, the paranoia of an old woman...* "Will do. See you in the morning, have a good evening." A tinkle of ice and the sweet scent of rum wafting into the lobby told her the old lady's plans for the evening.

Camera in hand, Gwen started down the street towards the nightclubs. Her room was small and the building run down, but it was cheap and close enough to the nightlife she could walk the distance. A strain of a saxophone solo sifted through the night from what was probably a club featuring a local sax player on Frenchman's Street. Most of the news reports and photos she had taken came from Frenchman Street. Whatever lurked there seemed to like it. Probably because of the number of drunken revelers too far gone to realize the danger before it was too late. A night in New Orleans always seemed to end in at least

Eternal Diet   *Wendy Wilson*

one corpse to be picked up by the cops. The homeless were in abundance as well and prey to all sorts of ills, not just foul play.

    Jasmine filled the air as she stood outside the club of the earlier sax solo. As she was about to go in, a flash of black appeared at her side. Spinning wildly, her hand slammed into the side of a clubber as they tried to go around her into the club. "Watch out, stupid!" His [very] thin companion laughed and chimed in "Well we do have to go a long way to get around her!" Both laughed lightly and pushed around her. Gwen bit back both her retort and tears.

    There was a reason she was here in this street with a camera. A reason why she jumped at flashes out of the corner of her eye. Down a ways from the club, in an alley between two small nightclubs, she had taken her first real photo. The very piece of evidence that convinced her she was on the right track. The thing she was searching for hunted on Frenchman and she desperately wanted to meet this phantom she'd been searching for. She wanted what the creature could offer her. She wanted eternal life and beauty; and eternal thinness.

    The feeling of eyes peering at her, boring into her skull slowly brought Gwen back to reality. Jasmine wafted again through the moist air carrying with it a

Eternal Diet   *Wendy Wilson*

faint scent. A remembered scent from when she was a child and had fallen off of the swings into the dirt. Only this scent didn't hold the promise of growing things. It contained the opposite, something dying. Or dead and reduced to dirt.

Slowly Gwen removed her hands from her face, raised her eyes to search the dark street. A darker shadow than the others stirred, and a pale face moved into view. A tall, beautiful, rock star in full costume. Black jacket on black jeans above onyx encrusted black boots. Long wavy light brown hair with a hint of gray at the temples and tied back against his elegant long coat. His hands were dead still, clasped together in front of his slim waist. His face and hands glowed faintly as the blackness of his garb enhanced the whiteness of his skin.

Even from across the street Gwen could see his dark brown eyes staring into hers an expression of bemused inquiry in them. Gwen stood breathless, unable to tear her eyes from his face, unable to blink her eyes. Slowly he tilted his head to the side and lifted a finger in salute. She couldn't move, she couldn't breathe.

The door to the club banged open, and a party of noisy celebrants passed Gwen into the street. When Gwen looked back over to the street, the figure was gone. There was only darkness in that recessed corner. Camera cocked and ready to shoot, she started across the street. Every step brought her closer to that corner causing raised hairs on the back of her neck until she felt as if she had been the student in assembly where the scientist has a student put her hand on the glowing, electrified ball, and all her hairs stood on end. Only not as funny. Definitely not as funny. Most definitely scarier.

She reached the building and stepped up on the raised sidewalk. Why were the lights out here and not on the rest of the street? Suddenly the overhead lights flickered and came on, first the one over Gwen's head and then the one illuminating the corner. Almost as if someone had released a dampening field. Shades of Harry Potter! Did someone, something, have a deluminator?

She was scolding herself for letting her imagination get the better of her. *So, the guy was dressed in all black, and his skin looked pale. Lots of dudes dress like that, and maybe he's of Nordic ancestry, do ya think? Why the intense look? And what was with the little salute and nod? Some clown trying to give himself a laugh over the fat girl falling for him? Probably. Yeah, most definitely. Time to go home.* She stepped off the sidewalk and started home. As she passed an alley, she paused and snapped a picture. Never know what might be in there.

"Why do you follow me?" It came out of nowhere; a voice so low Gwen wasn't sure she heard it.

"What?"

"I asked; why do you dog my steps?" This time the voice was right next to her. She jumped and turned. There he was, not two feet away from her, his voice low and insistent. "You have been following me for some time now. I want to know why."

"Um, um, um…" Now she was face to face with the man from the photos; unable to speak. "This is gonna sound stupid but I…I…I think you're a vampire" Gwen rushed into it. "I mean, all of the evidence points to it, bloodless crime scenes, mysterious actions…" She looked at his face, half expecting to see him break into a loud guffaw. When she put it that way, it did sound stupid even to herself. Instead, his eyes bored deeply into her.

"And if you think this, why do you not run?"

"Because I'm not an evil person, I'm just an ordinary working girl?"

"And this protects you?" Suddenly all of the books and websites and magazine articles felt like very little protection from what she saw in his eyes. He stepped closer and reached for her, forcing her deeper into the alley. Gwen froze, unable to draw a breath to scream.

"You stupid girl!" he hissed. "You stupid, stupid girl!" He pushed her rudely away and stepped back. At five foot two [if she lied about a half inch] Gwen was not the tallest person, and she realized her perception of his height was wrong. He wasn't so tall at all; he stood a tad under five foot eight. The unicolor black suit and slimness made him appear taller. *How come that look doesn't work for me?* His light brown hair parted at the crown had escaped from the ribbon and fell across his face. Craggy cheeks dominated a diamond-shaped face with a razor-thin nose. His lips were curled, and she caught a flash of pristine white but crooked teeth. He stood staring at her, his body trembling, his hands raised as if to ward her off. "Oh, you stupid girl."

"You've said that a couple of times, I think I got the point. Are you?"

"Am I what?"

Gwen sighed as he answered. "Are you a vampire?"

The vampire, if Gwen was right, sighed and looked beseechingly into the starry night. He shut his eyes and shook his head. "Let me guess, you have read all the vampire novels, correct?"

"Yes, but I also did a lot of research concerning myths, etc. and I think they are onto something. Deep myths have a basis in reality."

"So why are you not afraid? I could tear out your throat and drain you dry in minutes."

Gwen swallowed hard. "So, you ARE a vampire? Can you help me?" The vampire blinked his eyes.

His mouth fell open. "You want my help? I threaten to kill you, and you ask my assistance? Are you mad?"

"Not mad, desperate. If the stories are true, then great beauty comes with becoming a vampire. Look at me." She indicated her lumpy body. "I want to be skinny."

This was more than he could bear. He shouted; "You want me to turn you into a vampire to lose weight? Go to a gym!"

"I've done all that! It doesn't work. Look, will you help me or not?"

His eyes took on the slitted look of a predator,

"The books have much of the lore correct. Many of us do feed on the dregs of society and give a wide berth to the innocent. But not all. It is not a law, merely a guideline many choose to follow." He was suddenly uncomfortably close to Gwen. His voice came in a butterfly whisper as he bent her. "Do you still want to continue? Your blood smells so very sweet."

"Wait!" Gwen cried. "I have questions before I commit."

"Be careful. You test my patience. Be glad I have already fed tonight, and your audacity intrigues me. Come; let us go somewhere a bit more private." Gwen hesitated as the vampire turned deeper into the alley. "I promise to listen to your questions girl! Come."

"But will you answer them?" He stopped dead, raising his head to the sky like an exasperated parent looking for a solution to the pestering of a querulous preschooler.

"Yes. I will answer your questions. You have intrigued me for some time now, and I have questions of my own." Gwen followed him into the alley wondering just what questions a vampire might have for an overweight contract researcher.

"First, perhaps introductions are in order." He flourished his hand into a few circles and nodded his head. "My name is Colin."

"Just Colin? No last name?"

"Not now. It is your turn, Gwen."

"My name is… but you already know my name? How?" A smile played over his lips; a flash of white tooth showed turning it a touch sinister.

"Oh, I know a bit more than you know. That is why you are still alive." With a little shooing gesture, he said, "Go on though. I wish to know how you live your life."

"Well, you already know my name. I was born...." Colin interrupted.

"No, no, no. I do not want to know your entire life history, just how you live in this world. And how you came to believe I would help you."

"All right. I work for a business that does research for companies on a contract basis. My job is to access all sorts of different databases." At Colin's confused look she elaborated. "A database is a computerized collection of related information put into a certain order so accessing is simplified."

"Ah, much like a file cabinet in an office. Yes, yes, go on."

"That's it. Pretty much my life. I look up stuff for other people. My turn to ask. You seem to already know about me. How? And why?"

"Unlike every other mortal in this city, you alone, seem to be aware. Aware and not afraid. I find you intriguing." Another smile played on his lips, this one not so scary. "And your apartment is not as secure as you would like to believe."

"I KNEW I had latched the deadbolt!" A chill spread down her spine. Colin had been in her apartment.

"Does that information frighten you? It should you know. I am not the only one of my kind in this city. But we linger here, and dawn is not far off. One last question." He twitched his fingers again. Boy, that could get annoying.

"If you turn me, will I be beautiful and thin?"

"You will be immortal and perfect." Colin turned to leave Gwen but spun back. "If I turn you then you will give me access to this computer age we live in?"

"Yes."

"Then we both have something to think about." He melted into the alley, as the first glimmerings of the morning started to climb up the street. Birds sang, and the mist spun away into rosy shadows on the asphalt.

Much to think about is right.

"I DID it!" Gwen wanted to shout and tell the world but instead settled for a little happy dance on the sidewalk. *I not only have met a vampire but survived and even negotiated with him. Negotiated a deal with a vampire! Who da man! Or, in my case; who da woman! One step closer to my dream of a thin, beautiful body.*

Chapter Two

One year earlier...

"Arrrgghhh! I just bought these pants a few months ago! And now I can't get them buttoned!" Gwen moaned while she changed her clothes at the gym. "Oh, to be thin like you, Reba and not have to worry about gaining weight!"

"It isn't really all that hard, Gwen. You gotta use your willpower." Reba's glib and already been heard answer sent Gwen over the edge.

"You think I don't try? You think I LIKE being fat? Let me tell you something, girlfriend, I get on that weight room floor, and I SWEAT. I sweat to Zumba, I sweat to yoga, and I sweat on the treadmill. Nothing seems to work."

"It might work a bit better if you didn't go to IHOP afterward and get the Rooty Tooty Fresh and Fruity special." It wasn't the right thing to say to Gwen, and she jammed her towel into her bag and stamped out of the changing room knocking into another slim, toned woman turning into the room.

"Sorry, sorry I take up so much space" she sobbed. The slim, toned woman looked at Reba. Reba shrugged, and the woman went on.

I'm not gonna go to IHOP, I'm gonna go home and have a salad. I will eat a salad. I will not add dressing. She stopped at the Food Lion and walked straight to the produce aisle. The selection of greens and veggies was incredible. *I could make a whopper of a salad with all this!* Wrong choice of words. A vision of a large beef patty covered with cheese, lettuce, onions, pickles, ketchup, and mustard on a sesame bun blinded her.

She knocked into a display of potatoes and sent potatoes tumbling down the aisle. The attendant ran over and started to scoop them up and place them back onto the display. Gwen bent down and grabbed a few, and for a second or two, they did a little dance with each other trying to set things right. "No, miss, don't bother. It's my job. I'll put them back. You go along and let me do this. Please." Gwen grabbed a bag of pre-made salad and ran to the checkout and took it home. Without dressing, it tasted as if she was grazing in a field. Just like the cow, she felt like.

Later Reba called. "Look, Gwen, I'm sorry for my remark. I know you try hard. It's just your choices aren't always the best. You've done the Grapefruit diet, Atkins, cleansings and a bunch I can't remember.

Remember the time you got the doctor to prescribe Byetta. He said you were pre-diabetic and it would control your insulin along with a weight loss side benefit?"

Gwen sniffed and nodded. "Um, yeah. I did lose some weight."

"Because you got so sick to your stomach, you kept throwing up! That's not the way to do it. Listen, I've heard of a hypnosis thing, some of my family has done it, and it works for them. I'll meet you at lunch tomorrow and bring you the flyer. 'K?"

"'K. I'm willing to do pretty much anything at this point." Gwen hung up, rubbed her red eyes and blew her nose into a tissue. She looked at the pictures on the wall and all the books lined along the bookshelves. The books of thin, beautiful people, given a book deal for losing weight, dressed in black and the books all dealt in the same subject; some non-fiction but most fiction. The photos weren't ordinary models; these had been picked for their resemblance to the current fad of pale, mysterious creatures. If only….

***

A few days later Gwen stood inside a hotel convention room. It had all the usual tacky décor; blue patterned industrial strength carpet with almond, or was it eggshell, colored walls spaced with floor length blue curtains. Set up in the center was a table lined with CDs in paper envelopes with titles like 'Memory Improvement" and "Fixing Depression." About two dozen chairs were set up in a semicircle around a small table with a whiteboard on it. Only a few of the chairs were being used; mostly overweight middle-aged women in too tight capris and fancy silk shirts. Several women of Gwen's age and one man occupied a few chairs. She sat on a chair in the second row close to the end and examined the handout from the chair.

Before long, the session began. Dr. Rose, for he claimed a doctorate, explained the process by drawing diagrams with arrows and labels explaining the diagram on the whiteboard. "Not everyone can be hypnotized, some people will not be able to release control to the point of accepting hypnosis and suggestion." Well, that lets him off the hook if it doesn't work! All he has to say is 'you obviously can't release yourself.' He then had them sit with their eyes closed and spoke in a low, droning voice about how some food was 'alive,' and others 'dead' and how they would soon desire only the food that was good for them. The session ended with Gwen not feeling different but determined to make it work.

***

Eternal Diet   *Wendy Wilson*

Since the directions said to listen to the CD, he gave them while going to sleep, she dutifully turned on the CD player and set the volume low but high enough to hear. She climbed into her single bed and closed her eyes.

The bedroom was dark; only the blue digital display on her radio alarm clock broke the blackness. A dark mist swirled around her bare feet. *What the he..., where'd this fog... why am I standing?* Gently, like a slow flap of a butterfly wing, the air stirred, bringing with it the faint sound of someone breathing. Right next to her. The breeze stirred her hair and a strand lifted away from her neck. She closed her eyes and listened to the breath come closer to her. Deep breaths filled her lungs, she could smell something. Something not quite familiar, a hint of something of the earth, of dirt. A sense of deep, deep sleep, like eternal rest, came over her as the butterfly touch reached her neck. Gwen leaned into the touch and...

I WANNA HOLD YOUR HAND! I WANNA HOLD YOUR HAND! I WANNA HOLD YOUR HAND. The final chords of the Beatles first big hit in America blasted from the alarm clock radio. Gwen dove for the clock, slammed the button and snapped on the lamp. Her breath coming in fast gulps, she looked at her room. No one was there. She ran to the window, and yes, it was undisturbed. She had closed it. She was totally alone.

Breakfast was a banana, and a cup of coffee, not enough but willpower had to start somewhere, didn't it? During the drive to work, Gwen twice ran a yellow light and nearly turned onto a one-way street before finally turning into the office parking lot. Several motorists shook their fists, and one gave her the finger. Juggling the travel mug and pocketbook, she tried to catch the elevator before it closed. "C'mon, hurry up. Run!" She managed to make it as the door closed and squeezed in.

A whisper in the back "Hope we can make it off the ground." Gwen stared stoically before her. First floor, second floor. "My stop" and the voice of the whisper got off. At the third floor, Gwen exited.

Row after row after row of desks with computer terminals firing up for the day filled the large room. Voices called to each other;

"G'mornin' Susan-."

"Did you see American Idol last night-?"

"Omg, I NEED coffee-."

Gwen went to her terminal and logged on. Another day staring at a computer screen looking things up for other people. "So, did the hypnosis do any good?" Reba tapped her finger on Gwen's desk, "Hey, earth to Gwen. Did ya go?"

"Oh! Don't sneak up on me like that."

"Whadda ya mean, sneak up? I called to you from my desk, but you were in LaLa land."

"Sorry, guess I am a bit distracted. Yeah, I did go. Put the CD on when I went to bed and everything like he said."

"So, tell me more, don't leave it there."

Reba slipped into Gwen's cubicle and knelt down next to her. Gwen didn't know where to begin. "I, I, I don't know… something weird happened. It was the strangest thing; I fell asleep listening to the CD and just before I usually get up…." Gwen looked up at Reba with a wry expression.

Reba huffed "Out with it Gwen, what coulda happened that was so strange right in your own room?"

"I don't know how to describe it. It felt so good but scary too. Like I was doing something I shouldn't do, but I didn't want it to stop." She raised her hand slowly to her throat where the butterfly breath had brushed her. "It was the most incredible, wonderful…well, sexy, thing I ever experienced."

"Whoa! You're not supposed to get 'sexy' from a weight loss CD!" Reba glanced over Gwen's shoulder.

Their supervisor had entered the room. "Better go, El Comandante is coming. See ya at lunch."

Gwen and the others worked for a think-tank doing research for certain PACs requiring information to back up their decisions. At least the research she was assigned was easy enough to do, and most of the standard search sources yielded up the information the client needed. At a quiet moment, she googled: hypnosis and vivid dreams. Most of the stuff was new agey type stuff she x'ed out of right away. One article caught her attention; 'Hypnosis and Awakening Deep Awareness' dealt with hypnosis in some subjects causing them to become hyper-aware of things in the environment. A small percentage of patients undergoing hypnosis appeared to have a sixth sense turned on which made them sensitive to elements other people were not aware of. The author referred to it as "Becoming aligned to another dimension." Gwen printed the article and shut down her computer.

Reba joined her in the walk to the elevator. "What's up with you? You hardly spoke at lunch, and you plowed through that bologna sandwich. Heh, I thought you were gonna eat your fingers! You goin' to the bar tonight? Wade's singing."

"Got stuff on my mind. Listen, I'm bushed, gonna go home and vegetate tonight. See you tomorrow." Gwen clasped the article closed and hurried away.

Chapter Three

A bowl of nachos with chili and cheese later, Gwen was at her computer with a bowl of caramel popcorn and a bottle of Dr. Pepper. Lots of research demanded lots of fuel. She found the website with the hypnosis and deep awareness article and went from there. The first link redirected to a site dealing with past lives. No, don't think it was a past life. Next site was about spirit guides.

Link after link didn't seem right. One more try and she clicked, "Do you feel a presence in your room? It might be one of several entities…" Now, THIS one might have promise. Another bowl of popcorn, and three Dr. Peppers later Gwen decided she might have a handle on last night's events. Can it be? Can centuries of myths actually have a basis in reality? Are there really such things as vampires? Not the "I vant to drink your blood" type of Bela Lugosi vampires, but the silent, beautiful creatures who ensnare their victims' souls and drink their blood.

Website after website suggested at least some of the modern vampire fiction had roots in deep mythology. And deep mythology stayed with the human psyche for a reason; it was possible it was true.

***

After her night time shower, Gwen rubbed herself with the expensive body cream Aunt Amelia had given her for her birthday, paying particular attention to her neck and throat and brushed her long blonde hair. It lay limp on her shoulders. She frowned at her reflection in the mirror. The one thing on me I wouldn't mind having described as fat, and it's thin enough to see my scalp. Tee shirt donned, and teeth brushed she sat on the bed. Not gonna set the alarm. Let's see what happens tonight. She clicked the light.

The cell phone on the nightstand blared Reba's id tune of "Me and Bobby McGee." "Where the hell are you? It's quarter past nine!" Reba's voice was frantic.

"Uh, um...I...I...I'm not feeling well." Gwen stifled a yawn. "Yeah, that's it. I got sick during the night. Tell El Comandante I'm not gonna be in today, would ya? Please?"

"What's wrong? Do ya have a fever? Maybe you should go to the doctor?" Reba paused. "You didn't have another of those dreams, did you?"

"Naw, I'm just gonna give myself a day in bed. I'll be in tomorrow. Bye." She pressed 'end call' and set the cell on the nightstand. Did she have another dream? Gwen touched her neck, nothing. The window was closed, and there was no lingering scent of moist earth like yesterday. *Nope, I didn't have another dream. But I sure want to.*

What if these creatures aren't only in our dreams? Some respectable experts in the paranormal authored some of the research. What happened the other night was real? The scent of dirt was still there after I woke up. What if they can grant beauty and immortality to chosen persons? Oh… what would I do to become beautiful? To not be the butt of tired jokes? To be happy with myself? To become THIN? Would I do this? Do I dare? Where to begin?

Fifteen minutes later and coffee cup in hand a be-robed Gwen sat down at her laptop and fired it up. *Let's see, if modern fiction has roots in mythos/reality, then there are several places that might lead me to where I want to look into. Transylvania? No, too far away and too hard to travel to. Is Transylvania even a real country?*

Several more promising but unrealistic choices fell, and she was left with two prominent options. Seattle and New Orleans. Strong, beautiful, and incredibly fast fit both populations but sparkly vampires? *I don't think so. Not one of the myths speaks of them sparkling and what I sensed was not glowing, so it is either a misinterpretation or the author made it up.* New Orleans it is. She concentrated her research to New Orleans, and before she realized, it was time to go to bed again.

The next morning at work, Gwen could barely keep her mind on her assigned research, some boring political stuff dealing with statistics. Lunch came, at last; she hurried over to Reba and dragged her to the lunchroom. "I've figured it out!"

"Figured what out, Gwen?"

"Remember I told you I had this strange dream the other night? You know, the one after the hypnosis seminar?" At Reba's confused look Gwen laughed. "Oh, that's right! I didn't tell you all about it! At first, I couldn't figure it out myself, but now I know! The dream was about vampires!" She sat back on the seat and grinned. Reba just stared, a look of dismay on her face.

"Oh, come on Gwen! You can't be serious. Vampires are not real, they're stories made up to scare people. And besides, I thought you got over your obsession with them a long time ago."

"Nope, just stopped talking about it. Got too many looks from people."

She dragged out her folder and opened it to her first proof; a study on early mythology and early man's interpretation of the natural world around them. "It says here, by this professor, most myths are grounded in reality."

"It says SOME SORT of reality, Gwen. It doesn't say what you say it means." Gwen stood up and closed the folder stuffed with computer printouts and photos.

"I thought for sure you would believe in me, Reba. We've been friends forever."

"We ARE friends G, and always will be but you've developed an unhealthy obsession, and I am trying to be your friend by pointing it out." She put her hand on Gwen's sleeve. "That's what friends do, they stick by their friends, but when that friend is behaving weirdly, they have to do something."

"Behaving weirdly?!?! How can you say that to me? I'm no weirder than those professors who wrote all the stuff I found. You know what the only difference between those professors and me is? Do ya? They did field research. They went into those countries and interviewed people and dug up the facts!" She bent close to Reba and whispered "I'm gonna go do the research. I'm gonna find out for myself. Got my ticket to ride and I'm handing in my notice today."

Chapter Four

Not surprisingly, Gwen couldn't go to sleep when she got back to the boarding house after her encounter with Colin. The deadbolt was thrown and secured from when Ms. LaBeauf had apparently gone to bed. Too many ideas were twirling and whirling in her head. She lay down on the bed, jumped up again and started pacing the room.

Her cell rang, and Reba's voice jolted Gwen back to reality. "Hey Girl, what's going on? Haven't heard from you in for evva. You still alive?"

"What a strange choice of words, Rebe. Of course, I'm alive! What other option is there?"

Reba laughed. "Ha, ain't that the truth. Hey, sorry to be calling you so early, I know it's 5:30 in the morning, but I've been worried about you. Had a bad feeling all night long. Like you were in danger or something. Everything ok?"

"Me?! Nooo, I'm fine. In fact, I just made a contact that might move things along for me."

Reba hesitated, "What do you mean, a "contact?" You went there to research supernatural stuff. Vampires and ghosts and stuff like that." Reba gasped.

"Do you mean…did you….Nahhhh….you're joking, right?"

"All I can tell you, Rebe, is I have learned a lot. Gotta go gotta lot of planning to do. I'll call you in a few days, K?" Gwen pressed "end call."

Gwen sat down at her laptop and, grateful for the free Wi-Fi from a careless neighbor, turned on Google maps and explored the area near the nightclub for the 20th time that month. Hmmm, let's see, dawn came about 10 minutes after he left. Which means his place is a few blocks away at most. Taking into account his ability to move fast and what empty buildings are around, I have to expand the search area, access tax records… Light blazed in through the windows. The shadows shrunk and started to grow long again before she finally snapped the laptop closed and said, "I got it, I think I know where he is." She checked the clock. "I've got a few hours before dark, enough time, I think. But first, something to eat."

***

Her favorite café was crowded, but a few tables were still open, and she chose one out on the sidewalk. The waiter offered her a menu, and she studied it carefully. What had she not had a chance to try? "I'll take the crawfish with Maque choux please." She said to the waiter. "I've never eaten crawfish, but this is a day of firsts."

"Oh, then maybe I can suggest you have a Sazerac with it? You can't be in New Orleans and not drink it, Miss."

"Yeah, why the heck not." And she handed the menu back to the smiling waiter. After a luxurious lunch, and a Sazerac that relaxed her immensely, Gwen paid with the last of her cash. She went to pocket the change from the lunch and tip and then shrugged. Not gonna need this anymore, and dropped the rest on the table, grabbed her purse and set out down the street.

The café was a few blocks from last night's nightclub and a bit closer to her target than the corner of her encounter. Once off of the main drag, the crowds thinned quite a bit, and she soon found herself in front of the empty building her earlier search had uncovered. Katrina had done a lot of damage that no one seemed eager to fix. Much of the debris had been hauled away, but the building itself stood as a shell. Inside was gutted, with 2x4 wall studs all that remained of the partitions that once divided the house. Here and there were remnants of a better time, this house had seen glory in its day. The remaining woodwork in the form of crown molding was exquisite, the work of a fine craftsman. What remained of the banister to the second story was made of teak wood and was carved with intersecting Fleur de Lis designs by an artist with skill and feeling for his art. The old lady was stooped, but she wasn't broken.

Houses in New Orleans didn't have basements, so she started up the stairs. Scurrying mice ran ahead, their tiny calls rivaling the squeaks of the stair tread. Dust swirled on each step, and Gwen pulled a scarf from her purse and covered her nose and mouth. The squeaking grew into a groan, and the stairs began to shudder under her weight. She grabbed for the banister and pulled herself up onto the landing. *Whew! Don't know if I'll be able to get down that way.* There was a door at her left, and she pushed it open. *Empty. Nothing. So, what did you expect? A coffin in the first place you check? Way too easy.*

The shadows were beginning to settle, and the hallway with its closed doors was shrouded in darkness. The squeaking of the mice was gone and the birdsong from outside hushed. It was quiet, very quiet, the ubiquitous sounds of the nightclubs hanging in the very air of New Orleans were gone. Her keychain had a tiny penlight flashlight made more for finding the keyhole of a car on a dark night, but it was all she had, and she snapped it on. A thin ray of light pierced the blackness and disappeared 6 feet away.

C'mon Gwen, you wanted this, buck up and get going. Gulping down a reminder of her lunch, she put one foot out. A loud squeal of improperly installed wood swollen with damp froze her step, and she dropped the penlight. "No no no no, come back here you" she whispered as she frantically swept her hands from side to side of the narrow hallway floor.

From down the hall, a little 'thump' sounded. Her throat went dry. She climbed up off her knees and crept down the hallway. Her foot kicked something hard, and she almost screamed until she realized it was the penlight. Relief flooded her as she flipped it back on. Blessed light. Now, which room.

First door on the left. With her hand, she gently pushed it and watched closely as it swung open to reveal a bathroom in which the fixtures had been torn out leaving scarred walls and holes in the floor. And no place to hide. The door across the hall was a small bedroom, also empty of anything but dust marked with the tiny tracks of mice and a few larger pads that Gwen figured belonged to cats. One room left.

She put her hand on the door, closed her eyes in a quick gathering of courage and pushed it open. It swung wide and hit the wall. A fairly large room illuminated only by the ghostly light of streetlights. But it was empty. Nothing in it at all. "What? What was the thump? Where is he?"

"If you are referring to the thump from earlier, then I believe it was this pretty little tabby here." Gwen twisted around, and there was Colin, standing in the doorway holding a petite calico kitten purring and rubbing against his arm. His eyes bored into hers. "Now, will you tell me why you are here and what I should do about it?"

"Ahk," Gwen coughed and pulled the scarf from her face. "I mean, you startled me. I didn't expect to see you there."

"Clearly. However, you do appear to be searching for something." Colin gently placed the kitten on the floor and took a step towards Gwen. She backed away as fast as her shaking knees would allow until she felt the wall against her back. His black attire melted well into the gloom of the room, only his pale face and folded hands were clearly visible. That and his eyes. Brown and lit by a fire within, they held Gwen frozen; a mouse before the cobra. "Tell me, what should I do about you?"

The lump in her throat threatened to block her breath, but Gwen managed to squeak out "You should remember our conversation?" A soft chuckle.

"Ah yes, our conversation from last night. Tell me, what did we conclude?"

"That we both had a lot to think about. That maybe we could help each other?"

"Yesss, I do seem to remember something like that. And have you thought?"

"Wha, what?"

He sighed and steepled his hands. "Have you come to any conclusion? Not that you have much in the way of options right now." He spread his hands. "I do hold all the cards, as it were."

Gwen took a deep breath and launched; "Here's what I think, you need someone to help you cope with the digital age. I'm experienced and talented in that. In fact, when I'm not at my job I'm what is often called a hacker. That's someone who can break into other computers and get information, and I know all sorts of security codes or can find them…"

"Enough." He raised his hand. "You may indeed be useful. Your part of the bargain would be to assist me in acclimating to this modern world. My part of the bargain would be to assist your entry into my world. Correct?"

"Yes."

"Then let us not delay." And he was on her.

Eternal Diet   *Wendy Wilson*

The fingers gripping her head were like frozen stone as he tilted her head to the side. Eyes once brown and now radiating red fire flowed towards her. She could not tear her eyes away for they held her tighter than the hands clasped around her. Slowly his left hand slid down her blouse and slipped inside around to the fastenings of her bra. She felt it open, and she spilled out of the cups supporting her breasts. "My, you will be a full feeding," Colin whispered as the last of the buttons ripped away, and her blouse opened to fall off of her shoulders, exposing her throat. A small gasp escaped Gwen when his thumb rubbed across a nipple. "You like that, I see." And he leaned down to suckle. "Feedings are so much more enjoyable when the meal's blood is racing." Gwen shuddered as his tongue circled one nipple and then the other. She could feel the hint of something sharp rasp behind the tongue sending her into an even greater spasm.

Time disappeared, didn't matter. All that mattered was this never end. When the bite happened, she didn't feel it. Her body melted, and Colin followed her to the floor. Her heart felt weak. All feeling left her legs and then her arms. Cold entered her, and she struggled against it. "No, no, no you aren't supposed to take it all…please." She felt herself slipping away, the cold growing. Gwen gathered her will and with one last ounce of strength, pushed against Colin's body. "We had a deal, damn it!"

Colin fell back on his haunches and shook his head. Blood spattered onto the floor, Gwen's blood. He growled "foolish mortal, since when do the undead need to honor deals with their meals? I am still HUNGRY." He rose and stood over her; once again paralyzing her with eyes like a shark in a feeding frenzy, curled lips revealing needle-like teeth. Suddenly, his eyes cleared and became brown again. He licked and uncurled his lips hiding the instruments of his dining. "You are fortunate this is a deal that benefits me more than a meal."

He kneeled over her and said with a little laugh "The next part will not be quite as satisfying to you as the first part, but you will be glad for it." With his tongue, he closed the tiny pinpricks still weeping blood. He was right, it felt good but not as good as the nipple part. Then he rolled up his sleeve and with a vicious movement ripped his teeth into his flesh and offered it to her. "Drink this." At first, she shrunk away, what, drink blood? But she was drawn to it and reached for his arm. He encouraged her. "Good, yes, that's it. Taste. You will soon find it better than the finest wine."

Her lips closed over his wounds, and she began drinking the blood flowing from his arm into her mouth. A feeling of ecstasy flooded into her as the vampiric fluid was consumed and surged through her body. She wanted more. She wanted it all. She grabbed his arm and bore down and swallowed and swallowed. The world was reduced to her mouth and the blood filling it.

"That is enough!" Colin pushed her away. "Do not drain me."

"I want more, give me more."

"No, my pet, you have had enough and more than enough. Other meals will come. Now we wait."

"Wait? For what?"

He smiled sadly and almost gently at her. "Why, your death of course. Did you think this was all? Did you forget we are called the "undead?""

It took a few minutes. A slow upwelling of unease in her stomach was the first sign. It grew and passed throughout her body, burning and freezing at the same time. Her limbs became heavy, and her head drooped down onto her chest. A great weariness suffused her; she couldn't open her eyes. The cold grew, overtaking the burning until she felt as if the world was made of ice. Pain lanced into her head. "Stop this, it hurts!"

"Too late, it has begun and cannot be stopped."

Her body spasmed, arched like a bow pulled to full strength and released. But the relief lasted only an instant. Another spasm, this time throwing her body into a fetal position, hands with a death grip on her shins. Back and forth her body was flung. Tendons stretched to tearing, bones bent to breaking point. Pain, pain, pain, there was nothing else, the agony was the world. Her stomach contracted, and she vomited up her lunch. Again, and again she vomited up all her meals until nothing; but yellow bile dripped from her lips.

"Is this over, is this the worst?"

"Yes, you have cleansed yourself. Now comes the becoming."

Panting, Gwen laid down onto her side being careful to avoid the mess next to her. Cold entered her again. But this cold was a refreshing, brisk, awake, feeling. She jumped up and started pacing the room. Colin looked on with a bemused smile. "This is WONDERFUL! I feel so alive! I never expected this." She ran her tongue across her teeth. "Wait, where's my fangs? Why don't I have any fangs?"

"Like most tools, they are kept in their case until needed. Don't worry, they are there. And you will use them soon enough."

"And my eyesight! I can see you as clearly as if it were full daylight! Wow!"

She spread her hands in front of her. Instead of the pudgy fingers she had seen all her life, they were long, slender and elegant. She lifted them to her face and began to feel. No double chin, no puffy cheeks, and no pimples. Hardly daring to do so, Gwen looked down at her body. Perky breasts stood out, no longer resting on a spare tire of a stomach. Thin thighs and slender ankles. No more thunder thighs and cankles!

"I have a waist! Quick! Get me a mirror, I got to see myself in the mirror!"

"A mirror? Do you not remember the stories? A mirror?" Gwen paused, *Shit! Vampires don't have a reflection.* Her face fell.

"You mean I can never see myself? Ever?"

Colin laughed. "Oh, I can't do it to you. I relent; I can't be that cruel. That's one point only some myths got right. We can be seen in a mirror. We just don't usually bother to. We change little as you know." Relief flooded through her.

Then a funny feeling in her stomach started, her mouth felt dry. The scent of something....coppery and salty wafted to her nose. "What is that wonderful smell?"

Eternal Diet *Wendy Wilson*

"That, my dear, is breakfast. Lunch and dinner too, for that matter." Colin bowed slightly, held out his elbow for her hand and indicated the door. "Shall we dine?" Genteelly touching her fingers to his elbow, Gwen giggled lightly and with her chin held up like some Countess in a Harlequin novel, stepped into her new life.

Chapter Five

Once out into the street, Gwen looked around in amazement. "It's as bright as day! I can see every little pebble in the sidewalk, every bit of grain in the wood, every...."

"Yes, yes. You can see. Now watch and learn." Colin turned and started towards a quiet part of the street. Crowds of partiers, well into their second or third drink of the night, roamed from club to club. He continued to walk, and they started to thin out. He turned into an alleyway between a deserted building and a nightclub. His dark clothes hid him from everyone but Gwen. She caught up to him and grabbed his arm.

"Hurry, I can't take it anymore."

"Be quiet. You have to be patient." He peered around the corner at the sound of voices not far away.

Two scrawny men, both obviously intoxicated, stumbled towards them. "Ya, ya know wot, Phil? *hic* I think thishh is the best haul we evva got."

His companion, dressed in khaki shorts and a red tee shirt smiled and tapped his friend, knocking him to the ground. "Hey, buddy, sorry 'bout that…c'mere, let me help you up." Both men fell to the ground dissolving into giggles.

"You're so so so right, Benny. The old broad never knew what hit her."

"Lesh ssshe what we got." Phil produced a handbag, the sort of bag a woman with lots to carry might have and turned it upside down. The contents fell onto the sidewalk.

"Wow, Phil, thas a lot of cash!" "Yeah, and juss look at these diamonds!"

Giggling louder Phil realized something; "I bet she figgered *hic* if we didn't see it, we wouldn't know she had it! But we knew better!" He leaned towards Benny and tapped his finger against his partner's forehead. "We knew all about the old broad, din' we? Been watching her for days."

"But Phil, your own gran? Thas not right. Maybe we shouldna done it."

"Hey, if you don't want any…."

"I've heard enough" Colin slipped out of the alley and was on them in an instant. His fingers circled Phil's throat and squeezed. Benny let off a little squawk before Colin's pointy boot connected with his Adam's apple and both men dropped. Colin motioned at Gwen. "Well, come here and help me drag them into the alley."

Gwen rushed out and fighting the urge to tear into the throats of the two men, helped drag them into the alley. "They're still alive!"

"Of course, they are, the hearts have to be beating for you to drink the blood." Pointing at Benny's throat, Colin said; "Bite there. Eat."

The blood was delicious, better than any "Death by Chocolate" she had ever tasted. Better than any exquisitely prepared entrée she had ever consumed. She slipped into a trance, the only thing in the world was the warm, salty, rich red blood pouring down her throat, suffusing delight into every cell of her body. The heart beneath her hand slowed. She felt a hand pulling her away. "More! I want more!" she demanded.

"A glutton even now!" Colin reached down and pulled Gwen off of her meal. Blood slipped down her chin. "You must stop before the heart does. If you don't, you drink in your own death. Wipe your mouth. I wonder, did you need a bib before? Come, we must hide the bodies and find a place for you to stay."

"I can't stay at your place? I know it's not big but…"

"You think that's where I rest? Ha! You foolish girl. I'm beginning to wonder if you are as clever as you made yourself out to be." The immaculately clean vampire dragged the bodies deeper into the alley and covered them with some old newspapers. "There, this should prevent them from being discovered too quickly." He turned to face Gwen, not a spot of blood on him, not even his lips or teeth. Gwen self-consciously scrubbed at her mouth.

"No, I do not reside in that tumble-down wreck I found you in."

"But my research showed it was the best place!" Her voice was indignant. "And you were there!"

"I was there because I followed you there."

"But, but it wasn't dark when I went in." Colin gave a little smile.

"It was dark enough for me." Then Gwen remembered a key but a relatively unknown piece of the lore; the older a vampire is, the less he needs to avoid the sun.

"You must be very old."

"Old enough." Was all he would say.

All the bodies walking along the street, warm and smelling of delicious blood nearly drove Gwen into a frenzy. If not for the strong grip of the vampire escorting her, she would have dove into the nearest group of people and torn them to bits. "Not now, you must control your urge to feed." He whispered.

Someone heard him and glanced frightfully at the pair. "Go on, she's a little sick, a bit off her feed."

The observer looked relieved and, looking up and down Gwen he leered. "I bet I can get her back on her feed. Give me a few minutes with her, and she'll be up for a lot of things…" Colin ignored him and turned down a quieter street.

"He thought I was pretty! He wanted to "do" me! Wow." Gwen giggled and hiccupped. "Lemme go, I can "do" him…"

"No, you are drunk."

"Drunk? But I haven't had anything to drink." She frowned. "Except for the Salcazar. But that was hours ago!"

"You are drunk from the alcohol your food had consumed." He explained. "In a way, it is like 'you are what you eat.' If your meal has had too much to drink, then the effects can enter you. Especially if you are susceptible to it."

"So why aren't you drunk? Huh? Answer me!"

"I am, I simply maintain better."

"So now I'm a sloppy drunk?" Gwen shouted, outraged. "Well, I don't need you. I can do this, this, all by myself." And she started to march back to the busy avenue.

Colin grabbed her arm. "Oh no, you don't. You are my creation. We're in this together now, and I have to train you." He steered her down yet another quiet street. "This way."

Gwen's head fell back against her spine, and her mouth dropped open as her eyes took in the elegant mansion Colin led her to. "This, this is huge!" She gasped as Colin leaned over and shut her jaw. "You mean you live here?"

"Well, live is one word." He laughed at his own joke. "I can think of a few others. Come let's go inside."

"But dawn isn't for hours yet!" Gwen protested. "I want to hunt some more."

"Little baby steps at first, little baby steps. Besides, we need to set up a place for you to rest during the day. I hadn't planned…"

Gwen looked at him sharply. "You mean you weren't going to keep your end of the bargain?"

The vampire had the grace to look a bit sheepish. "Let us say I was keeping my options open. But, seeing how things went, we need to make accommodations for you." He opened the door and escorted Gwen inside.

A vast foyer led into a grand hall with a marble floor on which stood a table large enough to qualify as a room all by itself. A crystal chandelier hung from an ornate ceiling medallion. Colin hurried Gwen past the room and pushed a small rosette in the elaborate molding surrounding a mirror. A little 'click' and a panel swung open, and the two stepped through the opening.

"What! You have a basement?! I thought no building in New Orleans had a basement."

"What better hiding place than a place that shouldn't exist? It happens this house is built on a piece of property a little bit higher than the others. You probably did not also notice the first floor is raised a bit. Not much, mind you. Just enough to give a little more room beneath."

A candle and matches stood ready on a small shelf. Their light illuminated the stairs, and just beyond the foot, Gwen could see a small room. "This room was constructed long ago to my specifications. This house is far enough away from the water, so it rarely floods. The walls are waterproof, and drains are in place to shunt any moisture away from here. Even Katrina didn't affect me. We are quite safe and dry." The vampire wasn't kidding. The room was dry with no evidence of moisture having ever leaked in. It was small, about 12x12. Sitting in the middle of the room was the coffin.

Not your ordinary, mass-produced coffin. This one was gorgeous; if a coffin can be described as a work of art. It was maple with a rare pattern called 'zebra stripes' throughout. The craftsmanship was superb, corners dovetail joined so cleverly you couldn't see where the one piece ended and the other began. It had an old-fashioned one-piece lid and on the sides were oversized bronze handles. "I only have the one, so we will have to devise some place for you to rest."

"Couldn't we both fit in it? I mean, look at it, it's massive! It could easily fit us both."

"Impossible. I have another plan. Stay down here while I go upstairs."

For the first time since her turning, Gwen had a chance to sit quietly and ponder the day's events. *It worked! I'm thin and sexy and desirable and....* A voice intruded in her head. 'Stop it, you are not the first to experience a positive change in appearance! Come help me.'

Gwen gasped and slapped her ear. Wha...? Who's that?

Colin's voice answered in her head. 'So, you didn't learn everything about vampires did you.'

Indignant pride made her jump up and yell; "I learned enough! It said the one who turned me would NOT be able to read my mind!"

"My dear girl, like I have said before, the lore is only partly correct. No matter, I have found something that will work. Come upstairs and help me get it down."

Several minutes and more than a few thumps resulted in a lovely six-foot cedar chest lying next to the elaborate coffin. "There are blankets and pillows inside. It will do for now until you can find something more to your liking." Gwen slid her hand along the finely sanded smooth wood.

"It will do nicely. In fact, maybe it will do for good, I certainly will fit. It looks like they used Tung oil to finish it and cedar is a beautiful scent to sleep with."

"Suit yourself. There are other preparations I must make while you get your 'bed' ready." With that, he went back up the steps leaving Gwen to fluff up the pillows and fold the blankets.

Later, after she had primped as much as she could, she went upstairs to find Colin. He was not in the house, so she amused herself by wandering through the mansion. It was every bit as elegant as she had glimpsed on her way in. Every room had ten foot or more ceilings covered with elaborate carvings and molding, the walls with sections framed with intricate borders carved by talented and inspired artisans. The streetlights shining through the ceiling to floor windows lit the room softly. Soft oyster shell paint helped to give a glow to the rooms.

Framed paintings hung on the walls of enormous size depicting beautiful landscapes and laughing hunting parties enjoying picnics or indulging in the hunt itself. Gwen standing, mouth agape in front of a particularly familiar painting of a boy in blue dress when Colin walked in. "Ah yes. I do love Gainsborough, a bit ostentatious but otherwise not a bad fellow." He flourished a small bag. "Come with me, I have something you need."

"You will have to gather more after this night, but I have dug up enough of the soil to hold you over for a little while." At Gwen's perplexed expression his exasperation erupted. "You said you had done extensive research. Or did you let a little fact of needing native soil to sleep on slip by you?!"

"No, I forgot. Of course, I knew about it. It's one of the most common facts known, I just got so excited I forgot. Sorry."

"You should be." He handed her the bag. "Sprinkle the dirt around the bottom perimeter and get in."

"Get in? But it's early! The sun isn't up yet." A yawn startled her. "I guess I am sleepy. Aren't you going to rest now too?"

"Oh, why did I ever agree to this?" Colin appealed to the sky, or in truth, the concrete ceiling above. "Stop behaving like a naughty toddler. I am older than you; you are younger than me. I tell you when to rest."

Chapter Six

A ravenous hunger awoke Gwen. She had never been quite so hungry before in her entire life. *I wonder if I should have some soft-boiled eggs and…* A spasm racked her stomach, rejecting even the idea of eggs. And then she remembered. *Ah yes. Well then, girl, how about some type A?* That triggered a much nicer twinge, and she pushed open the top of the chest. The room still empty and dark. Colin's coffin closed, but somehow, she didn't think he was still in it. Draped over it were some women's clothes. She harrumphed. Black of course. But the delicate fabric and tight fit felt so good after all the baggy cotton oversized shorts and tees she had been wearing. *I can't believe I have perky boobs!*

A click from the top of the stairs and the secret panel opened. "Come up, we have much to do."

"How did you know I was up?"

A sigh. "You really shouldn't need all these reminders. It is simple; I can hear your thoughts." A few minutes later Gwen was up the stairs and gazing at her reflection in the floor length mirror that hid the cellar door. Looking good! She turned halfway around admiring the round little mounds of her derriere. *Hmmm, should I wear high heels?* Her stomach twisted, and her mouth went dry. The scent of blood and the bodies carried it was close. She had an appetite to appease. "When do we hunt?"

"The first rule of hunting is you do not talk about hunting." She looked sideways at him. *Did he realize what he said? Did he ever watch movies?* His next sentence answered her question. "The second rule, and actually more important than the first is 'you do not hunt near your lair.'"

"Lair? You make it sound like the cave of a monster!" Eyebrows raised he simply gazed at her. "Oh, yeah. I guess to some people that's kind of what we are." They locked the door and stepped into the New Orleans night.

The ever-present scent of jasmine hung in the air mixed with an underlay of salt. Gwen wasn't sure if it was a breeze from the Gulf bringing the faint scent or another, closer reality. She stood frozen, overcome with desire. "Not here." Colin's grip tightened around her arm. He led her across the street and into downtown. "Since last night's meal was regrettably close, we must travel a good distance before it is safe to feed." With that, he circled his arm around her shoulder and began walking fast. In an instant, the streetlights and club windows blurred into a stream of color and light. When they stopped, it was in a quieter part of the city.

Water lapped against the pylons of a private pier. A large and powerful luxury boat was moored at the far end. The water itself calm, the tiny ripples from the gentle current barely visible as they broke on the pristine white of the hull. The boat itself was large; about as large a boat as could reach this far inland. The bow was narrow and made for cutting the water at high speed. It probably had a fully supplied cabin, complete with kitchen, head, and bed.

From it issued sounds of a noisy raucous celebration, voices raised in drunken revelry and the BOOM BOOM from a state-of-the-art sound system. Colin grimaced. "Why must mortals turn the sound so high? First, they turn it high and then they yell to be heard over the music. Never mind, it is to our advantage. Come." And he led her silently across the boards of the pier and, waiting for wake of a passing speedster to rock their boat, the two vampires swarmed onto the deck. From below they could hear what had shortly before been a party had turned serious.

"Nah, nah Dubois. It ain't like that at all. I was just checkin' the stuff. You know, makin' sure its good shit." A cultured voice with a hint of Creole answered;

"I don't mind you sampling the merchandise; after all, it is yours once you purchase it, but you seem to be taking a significant amount from the package, and I have not seen any money yet."

"Gotta protect my investment, don' I?" A loud sniff and then a long sigh. "Yeah, that's the shit. Good. Hey Baby, wanna try some?"

A low sultry voice answered; "Just a bit. But save some for later…" Another sniff and sigh. Dubois was finished waiting.

"Now, you are both satisfied, let me see the mon…." The door to the cabin broke apart, and Colin and Gwen swung in. The first sniffer grabbed for a gun in a shoulder holster, but Colin reached out and with a twist of his hand slammed him into the corner of the table where he lay clasping his stomach and groaning. Sultry voice came up behind and slammed a bag of white powder against Colin's head and screamed.

"Leave him alone!" With a casual backward kick Colin cracked her knee, and she fell down screaming until Colin kicked her face.

Gwen was a second behind with her attack. Dubois struggled to get up from his armchair, his bulk prevented him from moving quickly. Gwen swung her fist and broke his nose. His chair fell with him still wedged in, and blood went flying. "This is much too messy. We have to hurry. Which one do you want?" Gwen looked at the three people lying on the floor of the cabin, moaning and trying to crawl away. Dubois desperately bargained "Take it, take it all. The money too." Gwen looked down at his plump fingers and double chin shaking and grinned as she licked her lips.

The realization these two had not come to steal the cocaine began to sink in, and Dubois redoubled his efforts to extricate himself from the armchair. "I think I will take the fat one." Colin took the other two.

"That was the best meal I have ever eaten." Gwen raised her head from the limp form beneath her. "So sweet he was probably diabetic. But I am still hungry."

"You can't still be hungry! That meal should have been plenty for you."

"Well, it wasn't. I want more. I want to hunt." They quietly slipped the bodies into the water; the current would carry them away and with any luck they would meet with a hungry alligator or two. The rest of the night was spent fulfilling Gwen's thirst.

Dawn was no more than a half hour away when the couple opened the door to Colin's mansion and turned on the foyer light. Gwen stretched languorously and with a huge yawn complained; "I can't wait to get out of these shoes! And this dress is pinching me too. I am exhausted."

"I am not surprised you are tired; we had an extraordinarily long night." Colin set his coat on the hanger and turned to Gwen. His look of sheer amazement rocked her. Gwen laughed.

"What? What's wrong? You look like you've seen a vampire, or worse!"

"'Or worse' it is! Look in the mirror, girl." She stepped into the hall where the mirror hung and screamed.

The mirror reflected, not her slim, taut morning vampire self but a doughy, sagging boobs body with a double chin and thunder thighs. Where earlier this evening a sexy young model with a body that was everyman's airbrushed secret fantasy stood, there was instead the reflection of the overweight, flabby woman she'd seen every morning of her adult life. "This can't be! How can this be? What have you done?"

"Me? I have done nothing. It was you who insisted on feeding long after your initial need was filled." He spread his hands at her. "This, this is all you, my dear."

"It can't be! Turning into a vampire was supposed to cure this! I was supposed to be thin and beautiful forever!"

Colin put his arm on her shoulder, he never could stand to see a woman cry. "There is one thing you can do." Gwen's sniffles dried away.

"What? You mean I can be beautiful again?"

"Of course, in another day or so you will be thin again and…"

"ANOTHER DAY OR SO?!? What the hell do you mean? Another day?"

"Calm down. In a few days the excess you consumed tonight will have passed, and then you will be thin again. After that, all you need do is limit your feedings." Gwen's mouth dropped open.

"You mean I have to diet?"

"Yes, my dear. Consider it your eternal diet."

Part Two

Chapter Seven

"C'mon, c'mon, answer the phone already." Reba tapped her manicured nails on the table. "Answer the phone, Gwen." The phone rang again and then connected. Reba pumped her fist. "YES! Gw..."

"Hi, this is Gwen. I can't talk right now so, please leave a message, and I'll get back to you as soon as I can. Bye. Beep."

"Noooo! Argh! Gwen, you've gotta call me! No one has heard from you in weeks. We're all getting worried. Day or night; call me."

Reba tapped the 'end call' button and put her cell on the table and looked at the faces around her and shrugged. "Well, I tried. Has anyone heard anything? Anything at all?"

"I got a card from her. She said she was having a blast." The slightly stooped brown-haired girl looked down at her hands folded on the table; "I know it's not much, but at least it indicates she's ok, doesn't it? I mean, if she were in trouble, she would have said, wouldn't she?"

Maria, a woman with short gray hair, spoke up; "Do any of us know why she went to New Orleans in the first place? Does she have family there? For that matter, does she have family here?"

She turned to Reba. "Do you know, Reba?"

"She's got a sister in Virginia I met a few years ago and a brother in North Carolina, but her mom and dad are dead. As to why she went to New Orleans I think I have an idea." The lone man of the group nodded.

"Yeah, I think I have an idea too."

"Then tell us, Willie," Maria said. "I know she talked to you a lot." Willie, a tall buff looking man in his late 20s smooched his lips and nodded.

"You know how she reads all those books about vampires and sees all the movies?" Everyone but Reba gave him a 'you can't be serious' look. "It's true, she always had one of those with her and have you seen her apartment? Covered with photos from the movies and magazines! She's obsessed."

Willie nodded towards Reba before turning his gaze on the others at the table. "You know I'm right. And she and I talked a lot. You're right Maria. I'm worried. I think she went looking for something we know doesn't exist, but she thinks does." He looked again at Reba. "And you know better than all of us, don't you?"

Maria waggled her fingers and widened her eyes before narrowing them into a frown. "This isn't real! And her wanting it to be doesn't make it real. More likely this has something to do with the kidnappings we've heard about." She looked at the dismayed faces. "It has to be said, sorry. Human trafficking is big business."

"Yeah. But," Reba tried to steer the conversation away from that topic.

"But what Reba? Don't tell me you don't agree Gwen was playing with a few cards short of a full deck!"

"What I believe doesn't matter. It's what Gwen believed; I mean believes. She went down there expecting to find some wonky stuff and maybe she did." Reba glanced at the clock on the wall, stood up and pushed her chair in. "Lunch is over, and I have to get back to work."

They broke up and started to walk back to their cubicles. Reba grabbed Willie's arm. "I've got to talk to you, I might have some insight."

"So why didn't you tell the others?"

"Are you kidding? Maria will pooh pooh the idea and Lily….well Lily is little more than a wallflower with as much ability to stand up to Maria as, as, as… that coffee mug!"

Willie quickly glanced down at the near-empty cup and then at Lily's retreating back. "You might be right but still no reason to not tell them. They were and are, her friends too!"

"You're right, but I still want to run it by you first, ok? Meet me at the Marina at 9:00 tonight." Willie nodded and touched her shoulder.

"I know you and Gwen were close, but you gotta accept she might not want to be in touch anymore. She's gotten our messages, hasn't she?"

"That's it, my phone says she opened the texts and voicemail." Reba put her hands over her face and rubbed. "I can't believe she simply doesn't want to talk to us. Not after…."

"Not after what?" Glancing around her, Reba leaned into Willie; "Shhh, not now. Meet me tonight, K?"

The Café parking lot was crowded; enough cars were parked to say even though it was a weekday, the performer playing was well liked. Reba opened the door and went in. Inside, Wade, the musician nodded and segued into Pink Floyds Wish You Were Here. He knew it was Reba's consistent request. His laid-back, summer at the beach with a mix of country and classic rock style fit well into the 20s and 30s crowds that were his biggest supporters.

Reba laughed and waved when she recognized the Floyd song as she walked to the bar. "Give me a Shock Top, please," she asked, setting down a five-dollar bill. Getting her change and the beer, Reba pushed the wedge of orange into the bottle and wended her way to a table in the back and sat down, waiting for Willie.

It wasn't long before the door opened, and Willie strode into the bar, dressed in tight jeans and an open collar flowered shirt. His black hair slicked back to best display his handsome features of black eyes, delicately feathered eyebrows, and full lips. Calls of "Hey, Willie!" "Looking good, Willie." came from both male and females around the bar and Wade did a little guitar riff.

A cute little waitress with a name tag saying "Hi. My name is Callie" asked, "Can I get you something special, hon?" Willie looked her up and down.

"Don't think I'm not contemplating it, honey." He winked "I'll have a Margarita, no salt." He sat down next to Reba.

"Why do you lead the waitresses on, Willie? You're never going to date them, and you know it."

"Aww, they love it. Keeps people guessing and who knows, it could happen. So, what's the story? What couldn't you tell me at work?"

Reba sipped her beer as Willie waited for his drink. Callie was at a table with a bunch of rowdy alpha type guys. She patiently waited while they pretended to peruse the drink menu. When she made to walk away with an "I'll come back in a minute…" they hastened to convince her to stay.

"Hey, don't run away. I know what I want, honey. Anything sweet will do." Another chimed in.

"Can you give us something sweet, baby?"

"I'm not your baby, and if you guys don't wanna order something right now, I'll come back later." She turned but just as she did one of the drinkers grabbed her wrist.

"Hey, pretty lady, you don't have to be cruel. We'll give you our order." He looked around at his buddies and put his hand on her butt.

Willie and Reba had been watching from several tables away, it was never pleasant to see a hard-working waitress deal with loudmouth customers, but hands-on was the trigger. Willie jumped up, knocking his chair into the next table in the process and strode over the table. "You guys have a problem?"

"Who are you?" Loudmouth #1 demanded. "We're just having a bit of fun, no harm done." He tightened his grip on the girl's wrist and smiled. "Right Baby? Just a bitta fun."

Callie smiled as she looked at Willie. He had a reputation, and in this bar at least the waitresses knew him and liked him for it. "Not fun at all, Willie. Not really." She jerked her hand away and stepped away. She wanted a good view of what was about to go down.

It happened so fast that loudmouth #1 didn't even see it. Before he knew it, his arm was twisted behind his back, and he was being frog-marched out the door. The door slammed shut on him as he lay sprawled in the gravel of the parking lot as Willie turned back to the table and asked. "Anyone else need a lesson on the proper way to treat a lady trying to do her job?" The remaining loudmouths suddenly discovered the menu provided beer and they all wanted one. Peace reigned, and Willie returned to his table; a grin of a job well done on his lips.

Reba took a deep sip of her beer and set it down on the table as one of the more experienced waitress brought Willie's Margarita. She paused for a moment.

"Thanks, Willie. Callie's kinda new and still learning how to deal with lowlifes like that bunch yet."

"It's a shame she has to learn then." He responded. The waitress nodded and left extra napkins before leaving.

Reba shook her head. "I don't know why you do that. Well, I guess I know, but someday you could get hurt running to the rescue. Anyhow, back to business.

"We both know Gwen was very interested in vampires." At Willie's raised eyebrow she rephrased "All right, she was obsessed with vampires. Anyway, the last time I talked to her, she said she had 'made contact,' whatever that means. And she was going to meet someone that night. I haven't heard from her since, and I'm getting worried something terrible has happened to her."

"I am too. Did you get in touch with any of her family?"

"I called Gwen's sister Emily, in Virginia. And, well, she said she had heard from Gwen about a week ago and she sounded strange. Almost as if she wanted to tell her something but couldn't. She was worried, talked about going to New Orleans herself to look for her. I told her to wait. Maybe we could help."

"I think we need to go Reba. First, no one hears from her and then the one person who does, says something's wrong. How much vacation time do you have?"

"A couple of weeks. You?"

"Almost a whole month."

"Good." Reba was glad to be planning something, doing something instead of sitting around waiting for the phone to ring. "It's settled then, we go to New Orleans. I'll call Emily. I'm getting more and more worried about Gwen. I wish I knew what she was doing."

Chapter Eight

Gwen sighed and took the mouse from Colin's hand. "No, you do not speak into it, you place it on the desk and move it around. See the little arrow moving? That's where your cursor is and when you stop over a blue highlight, and the arrow turns into a little hand pointing a finger then you can click onto the link."

"And that's where the information I want is?"

"Yup. You're getting the hang of it."

"And I can access information all over the world? In a few seconds?" Colin really was catching on to the digital age quite nicely. Vampires probably had to be resilient and able to learn new stuff to survive centuries.

"Yes, now you can see why I talked you into getting internet service here. We can't just walk around looking for Wi-Fi hotspots all the time."

Once Gwen had introduced Colin into the world of computers with her offline laptop, he quickly progressed to needing more than typing lessons and game playing. Just so much FreeCell a vampire can do.

It wasn't long before he was ready for the big time; the World Wide Web. For that though, he needed to get internet installed.

Now that was a tricky problem, the company wanted someone home, and they only came during the day, but a few calls to some local guys and some Ben Franklins waved about got them around the problem. What being rich can do! She had not realized the breadth of Colin's wealth until they discussed the need for a bribe and he casually waved her to a closet in one of the rooms and said to take what she needed from one of the boxes.

"That's my ready cash. Most of my assets are in real estate." He had laughed when he saw her mouth drop at the piles of cash stuffed in the box. "A vampire doesn't need much to live but to live well we need to acclimate to the local world. And here that means money. And, why I needed your assistance in learning about the modern world."

***

The jet set down on the tarmac and taxied into the waiting bay at the Louis Armstrong Airport. The "fasten seatbelts" light went off but most of the passengers were already up and reaching above to get their carry on. Reba and Willie joined the line shuffling forward off the plane. "I feel like that music video for

Eternal Diet *Wendy Wilson*

The Wall. You know, the one where all the school kids are in a processing plant slowly being carried to the grinder?"

"Ah, Reba, you and your Pink Floyd. Let's hope we have a happier ending."

The taxi drive to the hotel took them through the French Quarter, and Reba had her face pressed against the backseat window the whole time. "Wow! I think I saw Anne Rice's place! And there is Frenchman's Street." She exclaimed. "You know, the street Gwen talked about finding some interesting things. I hope our motel isn't too far away." A few minutes later the cab pulled up before one of those cookie cutter motels. This one has made some concessions to the romance of New Orleans and had decorated with a multitude of exotic plants and trees. A few small parrots hopped from bush to bush in the lobby.

"Reservations for Rey and Darling," Willie said to the man behind the counter. "And can you tell us if Emily J'sarajen has checked in yet?"

"Yes sir, two rooms adjoining on the second floor." He consulted his computer. "No, sorry, Ms. J'sarajen has not yet arrived. Here are your keys, the elevator is to your right. Will you be needing assistance?"

"No thanks, we got it."

Eternal Diet   *Wendy Wilson*

Reba looked worriedly at Willie. "She was supposed to have flown in real early this morning. Where can she be?"

"I don't know. Maybe she missed her flight?"

"Possible, I guess." Reba sighed. "Let's get settled in, I'll check my email to see if she sent a message and then we can look around."

Reba shut the door and turned to look at her room. Wow! Pretty damn nice for a cheap motel, it has a beautiful view and, she kicked off her shoes and fell onto the bed, a very comfy bed! Two minutes of luxuriating were all she allowed herself. Time to get to work.

She logged on to the motel wireless with her laptop and opened her email. There was something from Emily from her cell. "Reba, sorry I am not there at the motel but something came up. I think I saw Gwen and I'm gonna follow up. See u soon. P.S. I'm not sure if you know what I look like so here is a pic." The picture was a selfie of a slender young woman of about 25 in a bright orange tee shirt. Her hair was longer than Gwen's, and maybe a shade darker but the shape of the face, eyebrows, and eyes were enough to link the two as sisters. Shouldn't have any trouble recognizing her. Reba clicked 'reply' and wrote; "We got in fine, can't wait to meet. Where did you see her?"

She hit send and synced her laptop with her cell. That should do it, now to start the hunt. But first a shower.

She was blow-drying her hair when her room telephone rang. It was Willie. "Did you hear anything from Gwen's sister?"

"Yeah, sorry I didn't tell you right away, but she emailed and said she was here. And get this; she thought she saw Gwen!"

"Really? Did she say where? Never mind, tell me when to meet. In the lobby in 15, K?"

"K, see you in a bit." The room clock showed 3:22pm. Time for either a late lunch or early supper. She hurriedly put on a pair of shorts and a spaghetti strap shirt, grabbed her bag and locked the door behind her. Her phone rang as she stepped into the elevator, it was Emily.

"Hi, is this Reba?"

"Yes, is this Emily?"

"Yeah. Ok, now that we got the formalities out of the way, where are you?"

"We're in the motel just about to go out."

"Great, I'm at a little place on Frenchman's street. I'll wait for you on the street."

Chapter Nine

It didn't take too long to walk to Frenchman's street and even less time to recognize Emily. They chose one of the bistro tables on the sidewalk and ordered dinner. Or lunch. Whichever it was, it was delicious, and the trio spent the time updating each other on what they knew about Gwen and what might have happened. Emily related several funny childhood events, and Reba and Willie told Emily about their working together with Gwen.

Reba was the one to bring up the troubling reason they were all gathered in New Orleans. "Emily, did Gwen ever talk to you about the supernatural? You know, like ghosts and vampires and stuff like that?"

"No, she wasn't into that sort of stuff. At least not before she moved away." Emily took her demitasse spoon and stirred her espresso for a long minute. "Look, growing up on the farm, she was the one who poopooed any idea that something was supernatural. She was the one who would watch the scary movies and ruin it for the rest of us by telling how the monster was made by special effects! She always had an answer to all the scary tales too. Looking back now I can see how she wound up doing online research; she's a natural for digging up facts and not falling for nonsense."

"So you're saying she wouldn't go off halfcocked in search of something weird, right?" Willie steepled his hand hands under his chin. "So how do you explain her recent obsession with vampires?"

"What? Vampires? Ridiculous." Emily scoffed.

"No, not ridiculous. She even said she had photos of one right here in New Orleans. Photos she had taken."

Emily snapped shut her wallet and put the money for her lunch on the table. "We really need to start looking for her. She's missing, not crazy. While I was looking around here before, I got a lead on where she might have lived. One of the waiters knew her pretty well and recognized her picture. Seems she lived in a boarding house a few blocks from here." She waved a napkin with an address on it. "Got it right here, I was just waiting for you two to get here to check it out. Coming?" Reba and Willie stood up and tossed their money with Emily's. "Let's get going."

They walked silently, each lost in his or her thoughts and worries about Gwen. Finally, Emily stopped in front of a rather run-down two-story Victorian boarding house. They could still hear the music from the sidewalk musicians if they listened carefully. "This is it. This is where she lives."

"Doesn't look like much but let's check it out."

They climbed the steps and knocked on the door. The door curtain shifted, and then a querulous quivery voice said, "Whatta you want? The only room I got to rent hasn't been cleaned out yet. Come back next week." Reba rolled her eyes and yelled into the door

"That's not what we want to talk to you about. We're looking for a woman who rented a room here, and we can't contact her. Her name is Gwen. Do you know her?"

"Ya don't have ta yell. I'm not deaf. If ya looking for Gwen, then ya are talkin' bout the room." The old lady unlatched the deadbolt and opened the door. "She went out one night and hasn't been back for weeks. If she doesn't come back for her stuff by next week, I'm gonna sell it. You tell her that. Come on, I'll give ya the key."

The old lady stepped aside and fished in her pocket for the key. "She was a strange one, she was. Always leaving the deadbolt unlocked and then saying it wasn't her. Here's the key, toppa the stairs, turn right and first door on the right. I'll be in the front room takin my medicine."

Willie waved his hand in front of his face. "Whoo, did you smell her breath? I can guess what her "medicine" is!"

Reba grinned and gently punched his arm. "Shhhh, she's not 'deef'" Glad to have even a small excuse to giggle, the trio climbed the stairs and found the door. The key stuck a little, but finally, they opened the door to Gwen's room. Though it was only late afternoon the room was dark, the small window had its blinds pulled tight. Willie felt around for the light switch, and in a moment the room was lit. A small bed tucked in the corner, and a table with one chair was all the furniture the room provided. Scattered around the room were bits of wrappings and fries from a fast food place.

Emily went to the window and opened the blinds. "Yuck, twinkie. Old moldy twinkie wrapper!" She shook the the sticky wrapper from her hand into what seemed to pass for a garbage pail and wiped her hands on her jeans. "I can't believe she lived like this. I mean she wasn't the neatest kid growing up, but this is past unorganized. This, this is…"

"Messy? So obsessed with something that nothing else mattered, messy?" Reba was facing the wall opposite the window.

"Look at this." Emily turned and faced the wall Reba was looking at.

"What the hell? Who or what are all those things?"

"Those" Willie said, "are her obsession."

"But they are pictures from magazines and posters from movies! I don't believe that's what got her in trouble. If she even is in trouble. We don't know for sure. And let me tell you something, my sister wasn't crazy."

"Not saying she was." Reba leaned in and peered intently at one of the pictures. "This one doesn't look like a magazine or poster. It looks like a photo. In fact, it looks like it was taken by the café where we just had lunch!"

"You're kidding."

"Impossible"

"Nope, not kidding and it isn't impossible. Because there it is, there's the table we were at, and you can see the window curtains. It's the same place all right." The three crowded closer to see the picture of a white-faced black-clad man caught in the act of turning either to or away from the camera. His profile was clear if the rest of him was blurry. His mouth was partially open in a grimace.

"Can we see it any clearer?" Emily asked.

"Got a small magnifying glass on my keychain." Reba offered. She held the magnifying glass up to the picture. It clarified it quite nicely. "Oh my god." She gasped.

"What? What do you see?"

Handing the glass to Emily, she stepped back. "You can see for yourself." Emily held the glass up to the mouth where Reba had had it. The mouth was open enough to see the teeth. Not individually but enough to see any obvious flaws. And there was a flaw. A major one. The canine tooth was much longer than the others. Much longer and much sharper and there was something like a stain on it.

Emily backed away. 'That can't be what it looks like!" That's impossible."

"I agree, Vampires are only legend. But look over here. There's a couple of others. Give me the glass" Emily handed over the glass to Reba who studied the other photos carefully. "None of them are quite as clear as the first one but they are of the same man, and they were all taken locally."

"Look over here." Willie bent over the table covered with newspaper cut outs. "There are articles about dead bodies being found in the area. Seems like most of them are homeless men. One article complains about the local blood banks being a bit too fast and easy on who they buy blood from. Seems that more than one of those dead homeless guys had their blood drained from their bodies."

"At least we know what Gwen was doing." Reba sat down on the lone chair. "She was onto something. Perhaps she knew about the blood banks." She looked at Gwen's sister. "Would she be someone who got herself into trouble trying to uncover something like this?"

"Well, she wasn't a do-gooder if that's what you mean. But Gwen wouldn't let something as terrible as killing the homeless for blood happen. Maybe she tried to investigate." Emily let out a short laugh. "Ha, that was supposed to be MY line of work! I was going to be the investigative reporter."

The chair squeaked as Reba twisted in it. "I know she didn't bring much with her but where's her laptop? Nothing is disturbed, and there was some cash on the dresser, so she wasn't robbed. Her landlady said she went out one night without it and never came back." The others looked blankly at her. "So where is the laptop? And the printer?"

They started searching the tiny room, looking in the closet, opening the drawers in the dresser but no laptop. Not even paper for the printer. "It's like someone wanted only the computer, nothing else was important."

"You know, that sounds a lot like Gwen. I wonder if she came back for it." Willie whistled. "Hey look here, I found a flash drive under the bed. Did any of you bring a laptop?" Two pairs of feminine eyes looked back at him.

"I did."

"I did."

Chapter Ten

Down on the sidewalk across from the boarding house, Gwen clenched her fists as she glared up into the window of her room. "Who do they think they are, going through my stuff!" Colin's well-groomed hand gently stopped her from marching up and demanding an answer from the searchers.

"You no longer need that 'stuff' as you call it. You have retrieved the only significant item: your computer. The rest is unimportant. Attacking them now would only complicate things." He paused and looked up at the shadowy figures on the curtains. "I do wonder though, why they are here. Do you recognize them?"

"No, no, I didn't get a good look." She looked down at her shapely ankles and feet clad in expensive Italian leather and silk stockings.

Colin eyed her closely. "If someone has come looking for you it is best, I know now, while there is still time to plan what to do."

"It could be my sister and some friends from work. They haven't stopped calling me."

"Did you tell them anything? Anything at all about your experiences here? Did you say anything that might give them a clue as to where you are or what has happened to you?"

"No! Of course not! They didn…. I mean they wouldn't have believed me anyway."

Colin grabbed her. "Oh, you fool! If you have told them anything or left anything behind for them to find, then we will need to leave. New Orleans is not such large a city to hide from someone determined to find you, and I still need your expertise in navigating this new technology." Gwen stroked Colin's expensive suit.

"I got everything. They won't find a thing." *At least I think so. Did I have four flash drives or five?*

They turned and walked away, unaware that someone was watching from behind the thin fabric of the window curtain. Emily let the fabric fall back into place and turned around. Reba noticed her frown and, with a frown of her own, asked. "What is it? Did you see something?"

"I, I'm not sure…I saw someone who reminded me of Gwen, I mean, I had a powerful feeling it was her but. No, it couldn't have been her."

Eternal Diet   *Wendy Wilson*

She looked at Reba. "Did Gwen say she was losing weight? 'Cause the woman I saw looked like her except she was a lot thinner. And a lot fancier. And she was with a guy. Did she mention a guy?"

"Nooo, not that I remember. And you know she was always dieting. Without success, I might add. What makes you so sure it was her?" Reba asked.

"We're sisters, and we've been close our whole life. It's weird, but sometimes I know it's her before I pick up the phone. And once, I had a feeling for a week I should call her, but I ignored it. Turns out a close friend of hers had died, and she could have used a call from me." Emily's eyes opened wide. "And now I'm getting that very same feeling. Like she needs me. Maybe she's in trouble."

"I think it's time we go back to the motel and check out this flash drive. And," Willie looked sharply at Reba, "We need to tell Emily everything we know. It's time."

An hour later the three were sitting in Reba's room. She fired up her laptop and inserted the flash drive. Emily stopped her from clicking on the open files option. "Wait, Willie, you said there were things you two needed to tell me. Before we go surfing through my sister's private stuff you need to tell me why."

"We came out here to find her! Of course, it's important to check this. Reba, you tell her. You knew her better. And more importantly, you talked to her more than any of us since she came here."

"Ok. I guess I was her best friend." Reba turned to Emily. "You knew she was practically obsessed with losing weight, but did you know she did some rather stupid things?"

"All I know is she joined a few gyms and tried some crazy diets like the Grapefruit diet and a few others. What did she do that was stupid?"

"Well, for one thing, she got a doctor to prescribe Byetta. She did end up losing some weight but more because she couldn't keep anything down. I don't think even she would recommend bulimia as a quality weight loss method, but that's essentially what it was." At Emily's shocked expression she went on. "That was probably the most extreme thing she did, and she did stop, so don't worry 'bout it.

"I learned about this hypnosis thing that was supposed to work for weight loss and told her about it. She went and said she didn't feel different, but things started getting weird with her afterwards."

"Weird? How?"

"That's when she really started to get into the vampire thing. She told me she had some scary but sexy dreams…"

"Sexy?!?" Emily didn't buy it. "Sexy? No way. Hypnosis can do some funny things, but sexy dreams aren't one of them. Just what kinda doctor was this hypnotist?"

"He has a good reputation, works with a bunch of hospitals too." Reba sighed "Hey, I pooh poohed the idea as well. She stopped telling me about the dreams and started taking a lot of time off from work. I think she was researching vampires and started to believe the stuff she was reading."

Willie tapped the flash drive. "Can we look into this now? It might have some answers." Emily nodded and clicked the mouse on the open file option, and they all leaned in.

First up was a file titled address which looked like locations of various addresses within New Orleans. After that was something that appeared to be a search within the tax records going back at least 150 years. Next was one labeled "sightings," and she clicked on it. A bunch of photo thumbnails and a few videos opened up. They all peered closely at the thumbnails and agreed they were probably the ones pasted on the wall in Gwen's room.

"Check out the videos" Willie suggested. The first one was basically black with a few lights blurring across the screen. Gwen's narrative didn't enlighten them much.

"Here I am at the scene of the crime. The news said the homeless guy probably had donated blood and just didn't stop bleeding. They say the alcohol had thinned his blood. But that doesn't account for the lack of blood where he was found." The camera swung around, and Gwen' face filled the screen. "Damn! I didn't have the light on." A voice off-screen told her to leave that this was a crime scene and civilians were not allowed to loiter. Gwen's voice answered, "Ok officer." and the clip ended.

The next five or six videos were similar except this time Gwen remembered to turn on the camera light. They showed a crime scene roped off with some bored cops watching as the body was lifted into the coroner's van. "Not much in these clips, is there?" Emily asked.

"No." Reba agreed. "But there are a few more. Here's one titled "proof" and it has a date of about six weeks ago, not long before she stopped talking to us." This one changed their mind about everything.

Gwen's voice came breathlessly through the laptop's speakers. "This is it! I got him!" The camera swung around to reveal a still plump Gwen, wide-eyed and wound up. Obviously trying to calm her breath she quietly crossed the street and crept up on a dark alley. She whispered her narrative. "I saw a darkly dressed man go into the alley and then heard someone yell. But only a short yell, like it, was cut off. I'm going to check on it. I can hear somebody in the alley, sort of like a scuffle."

She approached slowly until she came to the corner and reached the camera around until it shone in the alley. The dark man was crouched over a jumble of rags, his face burrowed into the clothes. She must have made a noise because the figure whipped around and for a second his face stood revealed, blood on his lips standing out from a corpse-white face. He snarled and leapt up. In an instant, he was down the other end of the alley. "Oh my god! Oh my god! Oh my god!" Gwen chanted. "I was right!" The clip ended there. They were quiet for a few moments and then Emily broke the silence.

"That was the man I saw on the corner. With the woman who looked like Gwen."

"That's impossible!" Reba cried. "I don't accept any of this, this, farce! That's what it is, a farce." She looked hopefully at her companions. "It's got to be a trick or something, right? Gwen made this for us to find and…and… Oh, I don't know why she would do it, but that's got to be it!"

"We can't discount it might be a setup." Willie agreed. "Emily, was Gwen, a good actress? Because in that clip she sure was convincing."

"She was a lousy actress. Growing up the neighborhood kids would put on pretend plays, and she could never get it, could never do the emotions right. No, I've got to say Gwen really felt she saw something in that alley. What it was, I don't know. But what I do know is he looked exactly like the fellow on the corner. The one with the woman I thought was Gwen."

"If that's the case then she might be in real danger." Reba shrugged and with a wry laugh commented; "If he followed us to the boarding house, WE might be in trouble."

Chapter Eleven

Colin kept walking faster and faster until he was little more than a blur. Gwen had not quite mastered the technique and had to call out after him. "Wait! Where are we going?" Which prompted more than a few curious looks from the small group of clubbers standing on the sidewalk. Who was that lady calling to?

"Hey cutie, we could go to my place."

"Or mine!"

Gwen halted and turned towards the voices, her face a rictus of suppressed rage. These were the same two who had pushed her aside outside the club that night so long ago. She started to move to them, hands stiff and clawlike.

"Shhh, you don't want to do anything right here, wait." Colin calmly whispered in her ear. "We can deal with them later. Right now we need to make some decisions." They turned and walked away.

Voice one turned to Voice two. "Where did that guy come from? He wasn't there and then the next second he was."

"I don't know, but I need a drink. Let's go."

"Why did you stop me? I coulda wiped those grins off of their faces."

"There were too many witnesses. Do you want to give us away? Calm down. You will get your revenge, I promise. But we have other, more important things to worry about than two loudmouth louts."

"Sorry, I forgot when I saw who they were."

"Forgiven, let us go." This time Colin walked slowly enough for Gwen to keep up and when they arrived at his mansion, they wasted no time settling into Colin's lessons in the modern world. Several hours later Colin shut the laptop and declared it was time to eat.

"Finally! I am practically starving! I say we go after the two we 'bumped' into earlier."

"Agreed. Remember though, not to overdo it. You do suffer from a unique ailment, and the only cure is restraint. No more than one tonight." Gwen grimaced at his grin.

"Restraint, restraint, restraint! That's all I hear! That's all I've heard my whole life! Turning was supposed to cure me! Why me?"

"I don't know. I know of no other of our kind with your problem. And there likely is not much information regarding it on your internet. Come. They have had time to drink enough to be careless."

It didn't take long to come onto the scent of their prey, they had both had a good opportunity to place their smell firmly in their memory. This time, instead of Frenchman's street, the couple had chosen to hit the more glamorous places on Bourbon Street.

"Damn, this will complicate things. Too many people around to make a simple kill." Colin turned to Gwen. "We will have to make a better plan and not simply hope they come out at the right time."

Gwen peered into the doorway of the bar. "I'll go into the club and link up with them and lure them out."

"Don't take too long. I, too, am hungry."

Gwen laughed. "Don't worry, it won't take me long to get them to where they will get what they deserve."

She opened her little compact, fingered her hair into wisps of bangs and pouted her lips. "I love that I don't have to wear red lipstick anymore." Clicking the compact closed, she pulled the front of her low neck dress lower and wiggled her shoulders. "Do I look pretty?" Colin sighed.

"You look beautiful. Now go inside."

Eternal Diet   *Wendy Wilson*

Gwen glanced up at the sign proclaiming the club's name. "Yo ho, ahoy and avast me hearties." Colin followed her glance and chuckled at the irony.

"Shiver me timbers but don't walk the plank, bring them out. I'm in the mood for some buried treasure."

"Aye, aye, Captain." Gwen laughed and opened the door. The tinkling sound of glasses, voices chatting, and a jazz guitar solo escaped along with the smell of Creole cooking. The room was dark, a few lights scattered around the tables but most of the light was focused on the trio playing on the stage. They were playing a slow jazz number with a singer draped upon the mike. Gwen didn't pay much attention until she focused her listening to screen out background noise and pick up voices. Ooo! Can she sing those words in public?

Someone got up from a barstool and tossed a few bills on the bar. "Gotta go, work tomorrow," Gwen claimed his seat as the huge man behind the bar swooped up the money and wiped the bar where the glass had left a ring.

"What will you have, lovely lady?" He really was big, and unlike many bartenders, he looked more like his job was to protect the place rather than urge liquor on patrons.

"What's the specialty of the place?"

"Green Bombshell. It goes down smooth and cool, a lot like you." Gwen sighed. It was going take some time to get used to being hit on.

"You talked me into it."

"One Green Bombshell for the lady comin' up." Her neighbor leaned in.

"Pay that guy no mind. He's a jerk as well as not too swift. Won't last long as a bartender if he keeps that up." His voice rose on the last sentence to make sure the tender heard him. Gwen smiled into her hand. This was the guy from before.

"I don't mind. Too much."

"My name's Alan." He offered her his hand.

"Haven't I seen you around before?"

"I don't think so. I don't get to this part of town too much."

The singer launched into a new song; the lyrics even raunchier than the first. Gwen gasped a little. "I don't think those are the original lyrics to that song!"

Alan laughed. "I can see you are not familiar with this bar. Famous for it. That's why we, uh I come here." He examined her face. And then a bit lower. "Are you sure you haven't been here? I could swear you look like someone I know."

Eternal Diet *Wendy Wilson*

"Nope. Don't know anyone living in New Orleans." That's not a lie! Vampires aren't living. A giggle escaped her as her drink was delivered and she pretended to take a sip.

"I'll pay for that" as Alan flourished a wallet loaded with green. "Can't let you pay for your very first drink in this bar, now can we?" He let his hand land on her thigh. Gwen smiled up at him, all innocence and guileless. *Wait til you see what I have waiting for you, Mr. Laugh at the fat girl.*

"I have to use the little girl's room." She got up and waved her drink in her hand.

"Can't bear to part from this. Wait for me?"

"Sure."

Alan stood up and gestured for the other half of his pair to come over. A woman wearing a black dress painted onto her glided out of her chair and with hips swaying, walked over to Alan, waiting for him to speak. "Look, I've got a live one. Are you ready?"

"You mean that blonde you were talking to? I'm not sure she's what they are looking for." "She's close enough, she's drunk and willing." "Ok, ok. They have been pressuring us for more. But we have to be more careful, got a phone call from the station saying to cool it for a bit."

"We need the cash. After her, we stop for a while and let things cool down, ok? Madame isn't gonna be happy, but she'll just have to live with it." The fear in Alan's eyes belied the bravado in his voice. Madame was not someone you wanted to cross. Not if you cared to continue living.

Gwen dumped the drink down the toilet and flushed. She made sure she walked a little tipsily back to the bar. "That drink is the bomb!" She crowed. "Get it? The bomb!" She plunked her empty cup on the bar. "Bartender! Another one. And give one to my handsome friend here too." She realized another person was standing with Alan. "Who's your friend? She wants a drink too? Bartender! Make that three explosions! Ha Ha!" Alan and the woman exchanged a 'we're in' look.

"Sure, we'll all have another drink. Hey, let's go to another bar after this one. I know a sweet place."

"Sounds good ta me."

Gwen tipped the cup up and put it to her lips. She held it there pretending to swallow and then pushed it a bit too high. The liquid spilled over her and the bar. "Oh! I'm so sorry! Here let me clean it up." She grabbed the towel and starting to slam it into the spill making it splatter onto the drinkers close to her. "WOW! Thas some drink!"

"Come on, let's get you out of here." Alan took one arm, and the woman took the other, and they made it as far as the door before Gwen collapsed dragging them down. "Ah c'mon lady. Give us a hand here, will you?"

They stumbled up the steps and out into the street. Alan looked at the woman in black. "Whose turn is it?"

"I believe it's my turn." They started to guide her up the street. Gwen balked.

"No! Don' wanna go tha way. Wanna go tha way!" She waved in the direction of the alley and with bleary eyes asked

"Whose turn is it for what?"

"Just a running joke between the two of us." Alan held on to Gwen as she swung drunkenly towards her ally. "Ok, pretty lady, we'll do it your way. Down that way it is."

Gwen walked limply until they were at the entrance to the alley. She straightened and stood feet planted firmly as she pushed them into the alley. The two would be predators spun around. "Hey, what's going on?"

"Yeah, what are you doing?"

Gwen smiled slowly. "Remember that fat girl you pushed into the sidewalk a few weeks ago on

Frenchman Street? No? Didn't think you would. How about the woman you propositioned a few hours ago?" She waited. "No? Really? Nothing at all?" Colin came up behind the pair. They jumped.

Alan gave out a little scream. "I got it now! You're the idiot that was running down the street!" Colin placed his hand on Alan's shoulder to turn him. "And you're the guy who came out of nowhere!" Black dress tried to slink away along the wall. Gwen casually gripped her arm.

"You're not going anywhere, bitch. Never again."

Chapter Twelve

Reba opened the newspaper and scanned the headline. "Listen to this. They found the bodies of two people in an alley in Bourbon Street. 'Two figures in what is suspected to be a foiled robbery were found dead in the alley near the corner of Bourbon and St. Anne streets. They were people of interest concerning an unusual uptick in missing people in the city. Interviews with local bars reveal they were seen leaving a popular bar with a drunk woman, perhaps their target. Police will not give any more information except to say the loss of blood was significant. Police ask anyone with information, to please call 555 9503."

She folded the newspaper and placed it on the table and turned to Emily. "I'm sure it's got nothing to do with Gwen. There are thousands of tourists in New Orleans at any given day. Besides, it happened on Bourbon Street, not Frenchman's street. Which is where we're sure she took the pictures and videos. No need to get worried yet."

"I know." Emily sighed. "But it's hard to not get worried." Reba went over and gave Emily a hug.

"I get it. I feel like Gwen's a sister and I'm worried too." Emily sniffed.

"I thought you said there was no need to get worried." Gwen's friend hugged her close

"My head says that, but my heart doesn't always listen."

Breakfast at the motel was make-it-yourself waffles, bagels, cold cereal and a tasty assortment of fresh fruit and yogurt. The three friends enjoyed a meal before setting out. Reba clapped her hands together. "So, where should we start? Do we want to go back to Gwen's room?"

"How about doing the obvious and go to the police?" As usual, Willie's suggestion made sense and the clerk at the desk gave them directions to the nearest station which turned out to be not far off, near enough to walk and not take a taxi. "I'm getting to like this town; things are pretty close."

"But not so close I regret bringing comfortable shoes and not heels!" Reba wiggled her comfy sneakers.

At the station, Emily reported her sister missing. The sergeant asked them questions regarding how long since they had talked to her, and did they know where she was staying; the usual questions. But he then asked a rather strange one.

"Was your sister careless about who she went out with?"

Emily brindled. "What are you suggesting? Are you saying my sister was a tramp? Because if you are…" A firm male hand guided her back into her chair.

"Shhh, Emily. The officer isn't saying anything about Gwen's character. Are you Sergeant?"

"No, indeed I'm not alluding to her character. It's just that in this city, it's not unusual for visitors to get carried away and fall in with the wrong crowd. She will probably surface soon." The officer smiled a comforting smile. "Meanwhile, let me have the latest photo you have of her and I will have my men look for her." Reba turned over the pictures they had.

"Thank you, sir. You have our cell numbers." After the door shut Sergeant Beauparlant opened his cell and dialed a number. "You've got to tell them to be more careful. We just had another family member looking for a missing woman."

Reba skipped ahead of the others. "Well, that's half a day wasted." Emily slammed her fist into her hand.

"I don't like that policeman. Not a bit. He all but accused my sister of being loose!"

"Calm down. We never said we were going to let the cops do everything and us do nothing. But we had to at least tell the cops. They might be able to help." Reba made a 'not really' face at Willie. "Let's go to the alley on Bourbon Street. Maybe we can find something there." Willie shrugged.

"It's a place to start."

The clubs looked a bit different without the bright lights. They lost their magic without the blanket of mystery the dark provided. They looked like most bars in any town. Except there were a lot of them. And they were all open for business. Music trailed out of several clubs as they passed a few sour notes included.

"Sure hope those guys aren't the headliners!" They located the alley, a small ribbon yellow crime scene tape was still attached to one side, flapping in the breeze. Even in the bright sunshine, it was hard to see completely into the narrow alley.

"Paper said the victims were seen leaving with a drunk woman. Now, I wonder, why they were killed but not the drunk?" Willie pondered.

"Guess we'll just have to question the people in the clubs. Each of us have a picture of Gwen? Good. Let's split up and meet back here in a half hour. Emily, you take this side of the street. Reba, you take the other, and I'll take around the corner. OK?" They split up and started their search.

The first two clubs Emily tried didn't know a thing about the attack. Her efforts were met with sympathy but no real help. The third bar had a pirate theme. That sounds appropriate for 'shanghaiing' someone, and she went through the door. She had to wave to catch the bartender's attention. A huge, hulking man, more bouncer than keeper and the look of someone who has taken one too many hits to the head, was hanging over the bar peering dreamily into the low cut blouse of a woman who was pretending not to notice where his attention was focused.

Their conversation obviously had little to do with any drink she might order.

"Hey! Bartender! Can I get some service here?"

"Yeah, yeah. Gimme a minnit." Emily almost turned to leave but instead decided to play his game and wiggled her shirt a bit lower and leaned into the bar. "What does a girl have to do to get some help around here?"

That got the bartender's' attention. He gave one last lingering look at the valley before him and sighed. "What can I do for ya?" Emily handed him the picture of Gwen. It was of the two of them standing in front of the family Christmas tree last year. Emily grinned happily, but Gwen seemed to be avoiding the camera.

"Ever seen this woman in here before?"

"Yeah, the one on the left with the grin looks like you. The other one, not so much." Emily tried to avoid rolling her eyes, a more laborious task than anticipated. Leaning even further forward she asked in a low voice.

"She's my sister, and she's missing. Can you help me or not?"

The bartender looked longingly down her blouse. "Missing, eh? I dunno, wait a minnit." He scratched the back of his head as if the answer might be hiding in his hair. "Wait here, I gotta check with someone." He stepped back to the woman at the bar and held a whispered conversation. At one point the woman glanced at Emily, clearly suspicious of her. She shook her head at Hulk and Emily could hear her say

"...not sure….Madame…." Hulk came back to Emily still scratching his head. *Does he have fleas?*

"Sorry miss, can't help ya. Have a beer on the house though." He pulled a small glass of ale and placed it in front of her and leaned in closely. "She doesn't want me to help you, but if you wait until she leaves, I can help you find your sister." Now, why was there such disagreement about helping someone find her sister? Emily nodded and sipped at the beer.

Several patrons had come into the bar and the evening activity was warming up before the chance arose. As the trumpet did his scales and the drummer riffed and splashed the cymbals the woman at the bar got up and wandered into the back.

The bartender came up to Emily. "Do you still want to go?"

"Go where? I thought you had information."

"I don't have it. I know where to get it though. You still game?"

"Do I have a choice?"

"Yup. You can choose to not get the info. Or," Hulk shrugged. "You can come with me now. What's it gonna be?" Everything about this screamed NO, but no other leads had turned anything up. Emily nodded and drank the last sip of her free beer. "We gotta be quick," Hulk called to one of the waiters to watch the bar and grabbed Emily's hand and pulled her out of the bar.

Chapter Thirteen

"I'm getting worried. We've been watching my friends for days now, and except for the first day, my sister hasn't been with them. I know they came to try to find me and Emily fancies herself a detective. I'm afraid she's gone and done something stupid. Can we get closer? Close enough to hear what Reba and Willie are saying?"

It hadn't taken Gwen long to find out her friends had transferred to the boarding house she had stayed at and even less time to establish their routine. Colin would arrive first as the sun was setting. Gwen joined him after full dark had arrived. Together they watched the house and followed Reba and Willie when they went out at night. The lack of any Emily sightings was getting on Gwen's nerves.

"Shhh." Colin raised his finger to her mouth. "They are coming out now."

The door opened, and a worried looking Reba and Willie stepped out. "What do we do now? We've looked everywhere even remotely close to where we last saw her." Reba threw herself onto one of the ubiquitous benches found in the neighborhood and opened a pack of cigarettes. Lighting up she drew in the taste of the Camel Royal and sighed, her eyes closing.

"Since when have you started back smoking? I thought you gave it up."

"Well, I started back up, didn't I?" She barked. "Oh, I'm sorry Willie, my nerves are shot. I'm just that worried about Emily. No trace of her at all since we all went to Bourbon Street."

"Yeah, I can't believe that no one saw anything. Cops don't know anything, locals won't say, something's up for sure."

"I don't want to go back home just to say not only have we lost Gwen but her sister as well! Something is up is right. And I think it has to do with the number of missing people. We gotta get some help I think."

Reba looked around her, her glance seeming to linger on the corner where Gwen and Colin stood. And, even though he had darkened the streetlight, Collin involuntarily stepped more in-depth into the shadows, dragging Gwen with him. Reba tapped her companion on the shoulder,

"Willie, did you see anything across the street?" He peered into the corner Reba indicated.

"Yeah, someone might be standing there but the light is out, and I can't really see. So what?"

"That's the corner where Emily said she saw the guy standing next to the girl who looked like Gwen. The dark dressed guy from the picture." Blank stare.

"The one with the bloody teeth…?" Realization dawned.

"You mean…how could…why…you mean they are watching us?"

"Don't know what to think, Willie, but we've been finding out some pretty damn weird things. I don't like the vibes I'm getting from this. No weirdo's gonna scare me off." Without looking Reba stepped into the street. A car horn sent her flailing back into Willie's arms. By the time they had untangled and started across the street to where she had seen the movement there was nothing to be seen. "Will you look at that? The streetlights came back on!"

***

Several blocks away Gwen finally succeeded in dragging Colin to a halt. He coldly looked down at her fingers twined into his Italian silk suit and pried himself away. "Do not soil the jacket."

Gwen exploded. "Your jacket? How can you stand there and complain about your fucking jacket?" Her rage increased until it consumed any rational thought she might have. "Your suit?!? Your damn, fucking suit is more important than my sister? How dare you?" Passersby glanced at the stylish pair, the woman's behavior so out of character for how sophisticated she was dressed. Some onlookers looked ready to intervene. The situation had to be dealt with and soon.

The 'don't touch the suit' comment seemed to have sparked a deeper anger than Colin had seen from his protégé. Her voice rose until its shrillness injured his ears and spittle flew from her lips.

"You know fucking well who the "She" was they were talking about, and all you can say is 'don't soil the jacket'? My sister is in danger. You know it, and I know it. And so do they." Ice cold hands clasped hers.

"And the danger will only escalate if you continue making a scene. I apologize for the comment, it was unwarranted."

The calm tone of his voice and the firm way he took her hand finally penetrated Gwen's mind as he continued. "I, too, want to find your sister. But making a scene is not the way to accomplish it. Come, let's walk to the waterfront and enjoy the calming sound of the waves. Please." To the people gathered; "Her sister did not return home last night. She is worried, and I made an insensitive comment." One of the onlookers, a rough looking fellow, stepped up to Gwen.

"You ok, sister? You sure you don't want me to make this guy go away?" She forced a smile.

"No, I'm fine. Thank you for your concern, but he is a friend of mine." Ruefully she looked into Colin's brown eyes. "An occasionally insensitive one to be sure, but a friend nonetheless."

As predicted, the sound of the water helped to calm Gwen's emotions. The splash of the river as it swept by catching itself in little gaps in the seawall, the small whoosh of the wake of a boat as it washed against the pair and the gronk of frogs calling to one another plied its magic and soon she was able to think about Colin without feeling like she wanted to scratch his face off.

A little bit longer of gazing out on the boat traffic replaced her anger with sorrow. She took a deep breath and sighed. Colin felt her change from tense anger to acceptance and finally spoke. "You are an exceptionally selfish person. Are you aware of that flaw in your character?" Gwen sprang to her feet and stood over Colin, sitting cooly on the bench.

"Selfish!?!?! Me?!?! What do…I AM NOT! How dare you!"

"Oh, I dare much, and it would be to your good for you to remember who I am."

That sobered her up. She remembered quite well exactly who and what he was. For the first time in weeks, she felt a frisson of fear over what he might do, what he had done. What he was capable of doing. "So, where do we go from here? Are you saying it's time for us to separate?"

It was Colin's turn to stand. He stared out at the moonlight shimmering on the riplets of waves. The distant strains of jazz drifted from the streets, a saxophone solo sailing high on one held note lingered before breaking off into a riff of incredible speed. "You only think you know who I am. Your 'research' merely gave you a glimpse into the reality of what I am. Of what you have become.

"No vampire can afford to keep close ties to family. It is dangerous, and I have been foolish in indulging you in this. It has to stop." Something in his voice, the small break when he spoke of family perhaps, penetrated through to Gwen. She stepped next to him.

"You're right. I have been selfish. You had a family once. But you're wrong on one point. It doesn't have to stop. I can and will find Emily. With or without your help."

"Then let it be without my help." The slim, quiet vampire turned without a glance and disappeared into the New Orleans night.

Stunned, Gwen stared after the quickly disappearing figure. Her stomach growled, reminding her she hadn't fed yet. *What? Now? Now my stomach chimes in? I just lost the only person in town who can protect and help me, and my response is I am freaking hungry?* Her stomach growled again, a bit louder this time. *Well, guess I better eat. And screw the diet tonight. Tonight I feed until I can't drink another drop.*

Chapter Fourteen

Her first kill was easy and quick. She walked through the black park, pretending to be a little tipsy, a vulnerable single, woman all alone. Ripe for the picking. And it didn't take long for someone to pick up on her. Before she had gone a quarter of a mile, she sensed a presence shadowing her. Gwen stepped up her pace and listened. Yup, someone was following her. She stumbled close by an invitingly shadowy copse of bushes. "Ouch! Dam shoe, the heel's broken."

When the prowler attacked, she spun around and with a snap of her wrist cracked the neck vertebrae and slammed him down onto the path. Fighting the overpowering urge to sink her fangs in his throat right there in the open, she dragged the body into the bushes and knelt to feed. Wow, I didn't know I could do that so easily! Very little blood leaked out below the tangle of branches when she stepped over the body. A quick adjustment of the dress, a little brush of the hands to wipe away a few leaves and the vampire set out on the prowl again.

Eternal Diet   *Wendy Wilson*

"Mmmm, type O positive. I think I'll try for A or B. Or maybe even a diabetic? Nah, sweet desserts are for later, now is time for meat and potatoes!" A jogger running with a dog glanced at her nervously. Who spoke of blood types as food? His pace quickened, and the leash between him and the dog tightened as he looked back over his shoulder at the attractive woman wiping her red lips with her hand.

"C'mon girl, let's get out of here." The runner urged his dog.

Gwen felt great. A smorgasbord awaited and she was going to binge. Bet that guy doesn't come back to run here at night! Ha! She yelled, "BOO!" and laughed as the jogger ran even faster.

The next victim was chosen a bit more wisely and in a far safer, at least by vampires' standards, location. Alleyways were wonderful inventions. Especially when they ended in a dead end like this one. And with the lights blown out, it was absolutely the perfect setup for an ambush. Which is why the mugger was standing just back from the entry.

What the mugger forgot was that if you can set up an ambush, then you can be set up to be ambushed. So many don't realize that little tidbit. In her shadow deeper into the alley, Gwen giggled in anticipation. *sniff* *Hmmm, type AB, a rare one. A lovely*

Eternal Diet — Wendy Wilson

vintage from what I can smell. Not a lot of drugs, just some pot and while it is still young and insouciant, it is aged well enough to have a full body of flavor. Her victim heard the giggle and peered into the darkness.

A rat squeaked and ran across the lighter shadows, and he kicked at it. Just a rat. Voices carried down the street. Someone was coming. Mugger tensed, ready to spring. Gwen was faster. She grabbed him from behind, spun him around and hugged him into her

"Aw, get a room, why don'tcha? Geez, I know New Orleans is supposed to be easy but c'mon, doing it in an alley? Now I've seen everything." The voices quickly faded away as Gwen dragged her still struggling victim into the deepest shadows and sunk her fangs into his jugular vein.

Liquid warm salty sweetness exploded in her mouth. Gwen choked a little until she got into the rhythm, timing her gulps with the beat of the heart. 'Bump' 'gulp' 'bump' 'gulp.' Her nipples began to tingle, and a thin thread of electric pulse fired down from them to the space between her legs. Fevered fluid filled her mouth, coating her tongue and teeth. Too soon the flow slowed. Too soon the panicked look in the light blue eyes of the mugger clouded over, and his ineffective punches faded to spasms. Too soon the struggling heart began to skip, and when it faded to almost nothing, Gwen forced herself to break away. *Can't eat the last drop, that's death. For him and me.*

She knelt, her head falling back allowing her hair to cascade down her back. *Why is the second one always the best? Is it because I get so few seconds?* A few licks to close the wounds on the neck and bury the body beneath some trash and she was ready to find her next victim.

The police report the next day would mention an unusual amount of dead winos and suspected low lifes, but it was filed under "look into later, victims not important." Of course, it wasn't actually titled that way, but it might as well have been. Not all of the dozen or so dead could be attributed to Gwen, about half of them died of natural causes or possibly, other vampires working in the area, but Gwen finally was ready to call it quits in the wee small hours. Her feet hurt and her dress pinched in areas she didn't want to think about. She knew what it was. She had cheated on her diet, and now she was paying for it. Passing a shop with plus size clothes displayed in the window, she quietly broke in and 'borrowed' an outfit. "Ah, that feels better."

What do I do now? It's only an hour or so before dawn, and I need to find a place to sleep. But where? She looked up and down the street. There were still a few people strolling around, this was a city that truly never slept. Suddenly she saw the answer, at least a temporary answer. Across the street was the cemetery. And in New Orleans, a cemetery meant above ground crypts. And a cemetery as old as the one across from her meant old crypts which meant weathered and broken cement and access to the inside of the crypts.

Gwen shivered a bit, the idea of sharing a tomb with a withered dead body didn't appeal to her, but it was a safe place to sleep. A quick scout revealed several possibilities accessible from several avenues. Good, but it's still too early to go to bed as it were. What to do, what to do.

A familiar voice broke her reverie. "Willie, we're not going to find anything tonight. Stop for a minute, my feet hurt, and I need a smoke." Gwen looked down at her body, her old body and started walking towards the bench.

"Oh my god! Reba! Is it really you?" Gwen squealed with happiness only partly feigned. "When did you get into town? I can't believe it! What brings you here? Well, talk to me girl. You look like you've seen a ghost!" Reba and Willie sat on the bench, mouth opened, not believing what they were seeing.

Eternal Diet   *Wendy Wilson*

Reba closed her mouth first. "Gwen? Where have you been? We came to New Orleans to find you!" Relief and anger mixed at this friend who had disappeared for weeks suddenly showing up in the middle of the night acting as if nothing had happened. "Where have you been? What the hell do you think we're doing here? You disappeared weeks ago, you never answered your phone and the only texts we got from you were at best, cryptic."

"I'm touched you all cared so much for me, but I'm a big girl. I got some leads and followed them." Gwen smiled shyly. "And guess what else! I moved in with a guy!" That's close enough to the truth for me to be able to remember in a pinch. "Sorry I didn't get back to you, but I lost my phone, dropped it in the toilet. And, and well, you can imagine. This guy's fantastic. Guess I kinda lost my head."

Willie broke in. "You've had us all incredibly worried. Including your sister. Did you think of her? Did you know she came with us to look for you? And now you tell us you were just shacked up with a man?"

"Emily is here? Where?" It was hard for Gwen to pretend she didn't already know everything they were telling her, but the faster they got it out, the faster she could pretend she was just learning it.

"We don't know where she is. We went out a few nights ago looking, and she didn't meet up with us in the morning. Police aren't much help. Locals aren't much help. We're at the end of our rope."

Reba hugged Gwen. "I'm just glad we found you. One mystery solved. But I don't understand why you left all your stuff at your room?"

"Like I said, this guy's fantastic. He takes care of all I need." She snorted. "And you know the stuff I had wasn't worth worrying about. A bunch of blurry photos and unrealistic ideas. So, where are you staying?"

"Hope you don't mind, but we took your old room to save money."

Gwen smiled slyly at Reba and Willie, "Ahh, so the two of you are sharing a room? Didn't see that coming." She slowly punched Willie in the arm. "Didn't know it was in ya big guy." He blushed.

"It's not like that at all. We aren't…we don't…I'm not…"

"Oh, tell her Willie, she probably knows anyway." She looked at Gwen. "He's gay. And don't tell me you didn't suspect." This was news to Gwen although when she thought back at the lack of long-term female relationships among other factors, she started to remember about him, it became clear.

"I guess it is news. I'm not the most astute person when it comes to that, I guess. Oh well, now I know." She looked at her watch. "Whoa! I gotta go. Let's meet at Lafayette Square by the statue this evening around 9, and we can talk. 'K? See ya." The two roommates watched her go down the street.

"Something still smells fishy, Reba. I don't like this."

"Me neither. She just didn't seem so worried about her sister, just in a hurry to go. I hope Gwen's not in trouble. And who is this 'fantastic guy' she lives with?"

Gwen went as far as the corner and peered around to watch her friends as they turned and walked away. When they were gone long enough for her to be sure they had really left, Gwen crept back down the street and back into the cemetery. Fifteen minutes ago she had been all set to roam the city a bit longer, but now that urge was gone. Now all she wanted to do was crawl into a hole and cry.

Chapter Fifteen

Emily's heels kept catching in the cobblestones because this hulk was practically dragging her, and she was starting to think something was up. "All I need is some information, Bud. I don't see why we have to go anywhere." The grip on her arm tightened, and she struggled to break free from his unexpected tight grasp. "Let go of me!"

Bartender Hulk just held her closer and hurried faster down the almost empty streets. "Don't you make a noise. You want to find out about your sister?" the huge man snarled. "Then shut up and come with me. You'll find out about her, you bet you will." After that Emily concentrated on not tripping over the cobblestones and wherein this warren of a city, he was taking her. At the speed this guy was going and judging from his threat, he would have no problem picking her up and hauling her to wherever they were going, conscious or not. Better to remain conscious.

Even though the streets were pretty much empty, their progress caught some people's attention, and one man tried to stop them. Hulk Bud growled, "I'm an undercover cop, and this woman is under arrest for solicitation." That stopped the Samaritan, and by the time he realized undercover cops don't go about announcing the fact, Emily was far from rescue.

It felt like they went on for what seemed to be hours, Hulk pulling, Emily tripping along behind Hulk and trying desperately not to fall. The traffic on the road diminished as the road went from concrete to gravel to dirt until it was clear there were no humans for maybe miles. Emily had never been in the swamp but what she smelled and heard began to match every movie she had ever seen set in a swamp. Branches and thorns tore at her clothes as she was dragged along. Hulk warned her. "Don't try to run here, not unless you want to be a gator's dinner."

Finally, Hulk stopped before a large house. She was a grand old lady come upon hard times; proud of her past but unable to face the future. Along the house was a brick wall taller than even Hulk. Clearly designed for privacy. Muttering under his breath Emily's captor hugged her to his side and with his other hand searched the brick until he found what he wanted and pushed. A section of the wall slid open, and she was pushed through the tiny opening. Hulk came through right behind her, scraping himself in the process.

The grounds of the fortress, for fortress it was indeed, sloped upwards, towards a three-story gingerbread molded Victorian. But that's where the resemblance ended. The windows were all painted black and what looked like sniper blinds perched on the roof. No pretty curtains or lovely gazebos graced this house or grounds.

Hulk waved his hand toward the house and took a sidewalk leading to the rear of the building and stopped at a metal door. Emily could see that the entire bottom portion of the house was concrete and had no windows. A door opened, and Emily was deposited on the floor. Along the long side of the room were spaced what looked like cells in jail. Hulk keyed one open and with a mocking bow and a flourish of his hand invited her in and locked it behind her.

The finality of the clang did it for Emily, she broke down; she was scared and hurt and totally ignorant of what was going to happen. "What are you doing?" She sobbed. "All I wanted was some information!" Hulk's grin spread even wider.

"And information you will get." His laughter faded as he went up the stairs and shut off the light.

Emily allowed herself time to cry. Somehow crying cleared things up and made options easier to see. But not too long. She needed a clear head. She took a ragged breath, stood up and shuffled with her hands out in front. Three shuffles and her hand hit the bars.

"Ok, small space." She turned and shuffled at a right angle, this time she went a few more shuffles and barked her shin on a metal bar. Bending over to wipe her leg she realized it was a bunk and sat down. Whoever had set this up had planned for long-term incarceration of the inhabitants. "Why the hell did just ASKING about Gwen get me here? What the hell did she do?"

Chapter Sixteen

While Emily explored her location and options, Gwen slept the sleep of the dead. A traditional New Orleans funeral with all the music and wailing passed right by. Some of the mourners got a shiver as they passed the old crypt where she lay and unconsciously moved a bit to the other side of the path. Most of them attributed the feeling of being in a graveyard. But some of the grayer heads nodded at each other as if to say they knew mischief was not too far away. They kept walking though, there was another soul to get settled and no time to worry about what might or might not be lurking in the crypts.

The sun finally set with a slow bloom of reds and yellows changing to deep purple and finally the black of night. Gwen's eyes sprang open. She reached up to push the coffin lid. The sweet smell of cedar was replaced with the bouquet of decay and old flowers "Wha?" A groan as she realized all that had happened the night before. A quicker feel of her body reassured her she was the slim body seductress she wanted to be. "At least that hasn't changed. Damn diet. "And I forgot to keep my sexy clothes! Damn, Damn diet!" Only one thing for it. Find a woman of her shape and feed lightly tonight. Lots to think about. "Oh yeah, and that meeting with Reba and Willie."

Tonight was for hunting classier fare, so Gwen slipped quietly into the shadows doing her best to hold up the shorts that kept wanting to fall and trip her. A light rain fell as she began her hunt. Still, there were plenty of potential meals strolling the lanes, and she carefully homed in on a single woman standing outside a bar smoking a specialty cigarette. Her clothes would do fine.

Gwen started her stalk. Suddenly the door of the bar opened, and light glared out onto the street hitting Gwen full on. She stood revealed, a deer in the headlights. "The smoker looked at her and giggled "Hey girl, I don't recommend you wear those clothes here! You look like something my granddaddy's cat dragged in!" Gwen turned and ran.

"Damn diet!" she sobbed as she stumbled into an alleyway.

Luck was with her. There was a wino passed out, and Gwen swooped for the feed, unable to stop herself. His pants at least fit her, so she didn't trip when she at last finished and covered the wino with a newspaper. "Sorry fella, you weren't exactly what I was

Eternal Diet   *Wendy Wilson*

looking for tonight, but I needed your clothes." She walked out of the alleyway scratching at something tickling her crotch. "Oh my god! He had lice!" A few partygoers glanced at her and hurried away. "I guess you don't want lice either! Hehehe! I wonder if there is such a thing as vampire lice. Or are they vampires by the simple fact that they drink blood." she mused. "One for the ages. Gotta get a change fast," And she resumed her hunt.

At least with pants fitting she had the use of both hands, and it didn't take but a few minutes to locate what she was looking for; a shapely siren in a slinky dress. And just her size! As good fortune would have it, she was headed for a part of the street with an unhealthy [at least for mortals] amount of dark alleys. Gwen quickly went into hunter mode and silently sprinted ahead of her target and ducked into the same alley where her wino lay and stepped back into the shadows. Soon the woman was in range, and Gwen pounced. Within minutes a new body joined the wino, and Gwen had her sexy dress.

Running her hands down her perky breasts and along her dipped-in waist to her blossoming hips, she felt on top of the world. "Ah, that feels soo much better!" Giving her hair a fluff and her dress a final smoothing she stepped out of the alley. Somewhere a clock tolled 8 pm. Shit! Only an hour until she was supposed to meet her friends. Damned diet. She couldn't meet with Reba and Willie in all her vampire sexiness. To them, she was an overweight runaway they had finally found. No way was she going to let them know what had really happened. "Damn! I didn't think that one through. What do I do now?"

"You could feed until your particular metabolism asserts itself." Gwen whipped around. Not five feet away stood Colin holding her discarded plus size clothes, his head tilted and a satisfied smile on his lips. "I found these back in the alley and thought you might have a use for them." Joy, rage, amazement, fear, and sadness raced through Gwen's mind and finally settled on anger.

"You left me! You just dumped me and walked away," she growled. "Why? Because I love my sister?"

"Your love for your sister stood to threaten everything we are, and I couldn't simply allow you to destroy my life that way."

Gwen swallowed the angry retort she had on her lips. Colin was her guide through this new world, and even though she felt she knew everything there was to know, she realized she probably didn't know half what she needed to know. Face it. She needed Colin.

"So what's changed? Will you help me?" Her eyes hardened. "Have you been following me?"

"Yes, I have. I cannot afford to give into anger either. As infuriating as it is, we still need each other. I need you to help me navigate this modern world. And you need me to survive."

The clothes he held out were grimy and smelled of the crypt she had slept in the day before. "I don't want to know what some of the stains are. I can't wear those to my meeting!"

Colin sighed. "We can get you some new ones if you like. But we must hurry. That is if you have agreed to my suggestion." The idea of eating until she outgrew her lovely svelte body held a different meaning than it did a year ago, heck even a few months ago. Now overeating was solved practically overnight. *giggle* Well, over DAY! This metabolism of hers could be turned to her advantage.

"Ok, it just might work. I'll do it, but not in those ugly things. They stink. This dress will do for a while." A wicked grin grew.

"Now you're thinking like a hunter." Colin agreed.

Her first feed was standard fare as was her second. A means to an end. They employed an old but reliable technique of merely hiding in the dark until a lone prey 'animal' came too close and they pounced. "I haven't grown into myself yet." She ran her hands along her body. "One more feed should do it. I'm in the mood for a more exciting meal, let's go uptown a bit."

A light rain, more of a heavy mist, spread through the streets giving a halo glow to the streetlights but not much visibility. Even the music seeping out of the bars was muted and the chatter of the tourists passing sounded far away. Everything seemed to have slowed down, matching the ethereal glaze to the night. Gwen and Colin strolled quietly down Frenchman's Street rejecting one possibility after another.

"We can't take all night girl!"

"Don't worry, Colin, I can be a little late to the meeting. They're not gonna go anywhere; not when they just found me."

"Well, I need to feed too….OUCH! Don't grab me so tightly…!" He glanced down at the beautiful woman in her now too tight slinky black dress, her best "assets" trying to escape the top. No longer a sexy woman, she was now a lioness on the prowl, crouched and focused on her prey.

Swinging the little purse that had come with the dress and swinging her hips as much as the tight number would let her, Gwen greeted the lone man standing under the struggling streetlight. Colin didn't recognize the low soft voice as his protégé and looked around for what might possibly be a snack for himself. He gave a little chuff and watched with admiration as his student practiced her art.

"Hi, can you help a girl out? I was supposed to meet a few of my friends here tonight but I ran a bit late, and they must have skipped on me."

Her target, a handsome, successful looking businessman, vacationing in the Big Easy, smiled down at the gorgeous damsel in distress. "Sure, honey, what can I do for you?"

"Well, I've heard of all sorts of things have happened here lately, and I'm afraid to be here all alone, I don't even know where my hotel is!"

"Easy Gwen," Colin warned under his breath. "Don't pile it on too thickly. He's drunk, not stupid." Deciding to let this play out and observe his student's progress, Colin stepped back deeper into the shadows and listened. After all, his experiences with seduction didn't include males, and she was supposed to indoctrinate him into the modern world and that included social interactions.

She must have heard him because she changed tactics. Not the helpless kitten anymore she became the angry cat, all spitting and raised hackles. "I can't believe it! Those fuckers! I'll give them what for!" That went a bit too far, handsome businessman stepped back in surprise. "Oh don't mind me, mister, but this is the last time I get dumped and left by my so-called friends."

A long breath in and out and her composure returned. The mark's eyes were glued to her hands as she shook them in front of her bounteous breasts and slid them down the length of her painted on dress, just a bit too tight for comfort. "Thank god for yoga! Not only is it good for making me limber and able to contort myself into all sorts of positions, but the breathing exercises also help with calming me down." She side eyed the man, it worked; the '...able to contort myself…' comment clinched it for the target. He wanted to know just how flexible she was, and he didn't want to wait.

"Let's go somewhere more private. I know a place right around the corner." Businessman suggested.

The night air was scented with blossoms of a multitude of flowers wafting just above another, less pleasant odor of sour beer, car exhaust, and vomit. Gwen hung on Mr. Businessman's elbow and led him away from the main avenue. A fog followed and brushed against their ankles like a favored kitten wanting a snack. An alleyway opened on their left, and Mr. Businessman decided it was time to take control. "In here. Plenty of privacy for what I want to do." He pushed her into the alley. "How much?" At Gwen's surprised look he snorted. "You didn't really expect me to believe you were a damsel in distress, did you? C'mon, it was a pretty good act, I actually believed you for a minute, but I wasn't born yesterday! So what do you want?"

"Ha, ya got me. Don't worry, you have what I want." She took his hand and led him just a little further down the alley.

Businessman shoved her against the brick wall and pressed his body against hers. He really was a lot bigger than he looked and he kept her body squashed between him and wall as he caught her hands and forced them up over her head. Gwen's initial surprise at his moves turned to curiosity. With a flip of her wrist, she could put this fellow where SHE wanted him but decided to let him lead and played along. "No! What are you doing? You're gonna have to pay extra for this!"

Grappling both of her hands in one of his he reached down to her bra and ripped it apart. He pinched her nipple and pressed even harder into

Gwen. His mouth sucked desperately at her lips, storming the gates of her teeth. "Give it up, bitch, you know you want this." Gwen was dazed by the sensations threatening to overpower her, and when he slipped his free hand under her dress and touched that spot between her legs, she gave up a little moan, and her knees sank a little.

Suddenly he drew back and smacked her. "Bitch!" he hissed. "You little cunt. Just like every woman since Eve lied to Adam. I told you to stay home! Here I find you walking the streets after I warned you to stay home!"

That did it. Gwen shoved him down onto the filthy asphalt and stood over him. The look of pure amazement that a mere woman could send him sprawling devolved into fright when he looked into her eyes. And when he saw the teeth coming closer, he started to scream.

"Ah shut up." And he did.

As her fangs sunk deeply into his vein, a shudder went through her body from her nipples to the spot between her legs, warm and cold, painful and ecstatic at the same time. No sensation so powerful had happened before. At least not since she was made into a vampire.

THIS is what it is to have power over someone. Not just the swoop and drink; tempt them, make them so crazy they forget everything but you. Let a little violence season the drink. And seasoning it was. The blood bubbled around her lips and dribbled down his chin as the revelation struck. There was more to feeding than eating! The blood is better, pumps better, not to mention the other effects. She gave a little chortle and sucked even harder.

Colin was waiting for her at the alley entrance when she finally drank her fill. "Hurry, we must go quickly. You were not very quiet." He glanced at her, puzzled at her silence and laughed. "Well, at least it looks like our plan has worked."

"Huh?" Gwen shook her head to clear it. "What do you mean?"

"Look at you. You're pouring out of that dress. And not because it's ripped. Looks like you're ready for that meeting."

"Yeah, I guess I am. But not in this ripped dress. I need some nice stuff."

"I took the liberty of liberating a large caftan from, well let's just say SHE won't be needing it anymore. You are all set." Gwen put it over her ripped dress, a wettish spot near the collar caught at her neck as she pulled it on. Grimacing she looked at Colin. "I had to be quick, no time for finesse." She adjusted the sleeves, it was dark, and no one would notice one spot. Besides, it was one of the occupational hazards of her life now.

Chapter Seventeen

Lafayette Square was teeming with people. Flashes off of cameras sparked the night. Tourists strolled enjoying the soft air and their drinks, many still wondering at the freedom that allowed them to walk in public with alcohol. Many more were just taking advantage of the deal. It was hard to hear the jazz drifting from the ubiquitous bars over the conversations passing by as tourists went from one street performer to another. Gwen peered into the crowd. "I can't see where Reba and Willie are. You stay by the street and let me wander in here to look for them."

"Be careful what you tell them. You know very well they would not believe the truth. Do you have a story to tell them?"

"I'm going with 'found a guy, fell in love, sorry I lost touch.' That's pretty much what I already said so…"

"It will have to do; you are already late. Do not even hint of our true nature. And remember; I can hear you."

Gwen began a circuit of the park, enjoying the music and entertainers vying for attention and the five or ten dollar bill. She came back around to where Colin was waiting. She shrugged. "I haven't seen them."

"Maybe they had come and gone."

"I wasn't that late!" She tightened her circuit, getting closer to the statue. They had agreed on the statue, hadn't they?

Once again, she came up to Colin. At his questioning look she shrugged again, arms up and eyes wide. He motioned to her. "Look towards the trio and dancer over there standing in the shadow of the large trees. Do you see someone familiar?" Even with her enhanced vision, Gwen had trouble seeing what he was talking about.

"No, they aren't over there. Just some big guy standing."

"That's who I mean. He's been watching you circle around. Think, have you ever seen him before?" Focusing harder the guy's face became clearer.

"Now, where have I seen that guy before I wonder? You're right, he looks familiar. He's big and dumb looking, kinda like a bouncer....Wait! I remember. He was the bartender at that pirate-themed bar from the other night! Now, why would he be here?"

"Why indeed." Colin answered, "And does he know something about your sister?"

The trio of musicians and dancer finished their number, and the dancer nimbly leaned over, showing some luscious cleavage to its best advantage, picked up the hat and passed amongst the watchers. Every time someone threw in a bill, she danced a little step that bounced her assets just that much more alluringly. Her collection method worked well for soon she had the hat brimming. Time for a new number as the band swung into a classic while the girl danced along, her ballet training evident even though it was most definitely not ballet she was dancing. More people wandered over to watch. This group was going to do well tonight.

Just as Gwen and Colin were about to turn and leave, they heard a voice yell "Gwen! Over here!"

"I'll keep an eye on our spying friend while you talk to your friends." Colin melted away as quickly as only a vampire can.

Gwen swung around and there was Reba and Willie jogging towards her. "Reba! Where have you been? I've been doing circuits until my head thinks I'm on a merry go round!"

"Sorry, we took the trolley. So glad you stuck around."

"Yeah, I was worried, but I knew you wouldn't just blow me off. I am relieved though."

Willie gave her a hug. "Relieved? Why?"

"Of course I'm relieved! First, you tell me Emily is missing and then you don't show up. What was I supposed to do?" Reba leaned her head as if the noise in the park wasn't enough to cover what she was going to say.

"About that, we have a lot to fill you in on. There's a bench right there."

They settled in on a bench and updated each other about what had happened in the past few months. Gwen's story, of course, was heavily edited and limited to pretty much what she had already told them; she had found some interesting but ultimately useless vampire stuff; met a guy and fell head over heels in love, yadda yadda. As soon as her story had been told to her friends, she could tell that they didn't buy it completely, but that didn't matter; she couldn't tell them anything more.

"Like I said, I fell in love with this fantastic guy and moved in with him." Her friends' expressions

Eternal Diet   *Wendy Wilson*

were nothing if not dubious. "I see now my coming here was maybe a mistake and I should have kept up with you all but…. Well, I, lost my head, I guess. You gotta remember guys, I've never even dated steadily. And now I have someone who wants me to live with him!"

    Gwen watched as Reba and Willie mulled over what she had said. She hoped they believed her. What she had become really wasn't that important when you got down to it… what mattered, right now, was Emily. Where was her sister? And did that bartender have any connection to her. "Tell me what you've been doing since you got here. What were you guys doing when she went missing? Where were you? Where is my sister?"

Chapter Eighteen

Emily had no way of knowing how long she had been locked up, it could have been days or even weeks. Hardly any noise penetrated the stairs to her cell, but every once in a while, someone came down and brought her water and bread and took away the bucket she used for a toilet.

These minions, there was no other way to describe these pale skeletal beings, wordlessly performed their duties and didn't respond to her pleas. They didn't look at Emily, and she couldn't tell if they were male or female. They all looked pretty much identical with shorn heads and wearing shapeless smocks. What bothered Emily the most was their utter hopelessness and submission to whoever or whatever gave them orders. Is that what they plan for me?

One of the minions came down the stairs with her one meal. At first, she had eaten it all at once but by the time she was fed again she was starving so now she broke the bread up into several servings and hoped she saved enough each time. Only one this time. Which meant the door wasn't going to be opened to collect her bucket. She had tried to push past the minion the first time the door was opened, but the agonizing howl the creature made froze her and summoned a more intelligent guard who taught her that it was not a good idea. The bruises and cuts she got from him made the lesson quite clear.

Once again, she tried to get the creature's attention. "Hey, help me. Please." Again and still, no response. The minion slid the tray with the bread and water under the gate before turning and shuffling away. Emily took it to the cot and carefully felt the loaf and divided it into several equal parts before breaking a mouthful off of one of the sections. She raised it to her mouth and slowly put it on her tongue, chewing it thoroughly before swallowing. Another piece, carefully placed, chewed and swallowed. And another. A scraping sound of metal at the top of the stair stopped her in mid-chew. This was new. The minions had never come back so soon. Something was happening. The door was pulled open, and the light was flipped on, blinding Emily. Her hand raised to shield her eyes from the glaring bulb. Tears streamed down her face, whether from the searing light or terror even she couldn't say. Her heart raced as she struggled to see who was coming down the stairs. Heavy shoes and grunts accented the squeal of the wooden steps;

this was no ghostly minion. A gruff voice called out. "Hey girl, the Madame wants to see you. Ain't you the lucky one?"

Her eyes smarting to adjust to the brightness from the candles hanging from a ceiling looming high overhead, Emily stood in the doorway of what she could make out was a large room. The floor was well polished and intricately patterned tile, the type that in the olden days would be perfect for dancing the minuet or a waltz. She could make out a column stood close by, and she could see its partners dotting the length of the room, which was prodigious.

Heavy, curtains covered what appeared to be ceiling to floor windows allowed not a speck of light to shine in. Either it was night time, or they were very heavy curtains indeed. A familiar scent tickled her nose, she couldn't quite place it until she made out a tiny orange, red glow of incense sticks dotted around the room. Definitely not a flowery smell, they gave off just enough light to illuminate the small tables they were on.

As her eyes adjusted, she could make out shadows concealing the periphery of the room. Inside those shadows, deeper shadows moved beyond the reach of the light. The room wasn't really that bright, it was her eyes that weren't used to any light at all she realized. The guard led her to the middle of the floor and left. His sudden departure made Emily feel more alone than she had ever felt. He wasn't a friend, but at least he was predictable. And now she stood exposed to the shadows that surrounded her.

"Hello?" Whispers of snickers skirted the edges of the room, not quite words but almost words. Shadows flowed with the sound surrounding Emily. "Hello? Please? What do you want?" A voice whispered.

"What do you want?" behind her shoulder. She swung around but the air was empty, nothing was there. Another voice

"What do you want? This time in front of her. Again she spun herself around to see nothing but empty space. And the shadows moving closer and the voices defining themselves a little clearer.

Emily shivered. Her mind raced. What were these people doing? What were they playing at? Anger bubbled up "You have no right to do this to me!"

And from yet another shadow

"You have no right to do this to me!" Another voice, this time from the ceiling;

"You have no right to do this to me!" Spinning around trying to catch the voices and shadows as they flit by her Emily reached out and felt something dry and cold pass by and her mouth went dry...

"We have every right to do this to you!"

"Enough! You have played enough!" An imperious voice with the faint accent Emily couldn't recognize rang out from the far end of the room. In the deepest shadow, a curtain was drawn back to illuminate a tiny woman dressed in silken robes surrounded by expensive beeswax candles and seated on an ornate, throne-like, chair. Tiny slippered feet set upon a footstool. She gave off the essence of incredible age even though she appeared to be little more than middle-aged.

Embroidery covered every single inch of her pale yellow gown, images of tigers and lions surrounded by delicate peonies and plum blossoms. "Come closer, Miss J'sarajen." Emily took a step and stopped, confused. "Oh, I know quite a lot about you. One does not reach my position in life without knowing the world around and the people within. Come closer. I won't bite." The shadows around the room laughed.

The woman's jet black hair was sculpted to a high tower and was studded with ebony sticks and combs, which were in turn decorated with tiny, silver bells and jade figurines of phoenixes and endless knots. Her hands were folded neatly and correctly on her lap. The nails looked anything but correct though; they were hideously long and sharp enough to cut flesh.

The closer Emily got the clearer she could see the figure on the chair and the deeper her fear rooted into her gut until it was all she could do to put one foot before another. "That's close enough." Emily fought a desire to fall to the floor, she locked her knees and raised her head to meet the enigmatic woman's narrow eyes. Which were black; a deep, deep black that seemed to have no bottom to their depth and certainly no soul.

"I, I, I don't know why you brought me…"

"Silence!" The imperious voice projected to every corner of the room. The shadows roiled in the dark and sibilant whispers rose in the shadows, indignant and angry. "You are here to answer questions, not ask them…" She leaned forward and squinted her already narrow eyes. "I want to know why you are looking for a woman so dangerous."

"A woman 'so dangerous'?!? My sister, my mousey sister Gwen?" Emily almost laughed until she looked into the black eyes again. Eyes that were not laughing. "Gwen's not dangerous. She's one of the least dangerous persons I know. She's a mouse."

Realization dawned on the woman's face, "Ah, she is your sister! And you do not know what she has become" She tapped her fingernails on her cheek. "You are completely unaware of what you have blundered into." She paused, her fingers tapping her rich brocade. "This does change things. The question is what do we do with you?"

"Uh, let me go?"

The smile that rose on Madame's lips did not reach her soulless eyes. "You have a sense of humor. That will help you." She motioned to one of the shadows to come to her. A tall, pale man with flowing red hair and lips glided over and leaned in to hear her instructions. "Miss J'sarajen, I am sorry, but I will require your presence for a little longer." To the red-haired man; "Take her to one of the bedrooms and secure her there. I don't believe we need to keep her totally in the dark, do you?" Red nodded and with a grip as strong as iron escorted Emily out of the room.

Chapter Nineteen

Reba and Willie finished their discussion. They agreed they would not tell Gwen about finding the thumb drive until they got more details. They didn't honestly believe the bit about her "forgetting" to keep in touch. Something was going on, and they wanted Gwen to tell them more than she had so far. It hurt to not be able to trust someone who had been a friend for so long, but maybe Gwen wasn't able to tell. Maybe someone was not letting her talk. "Ok, here's the thing, Gwen." Reba took Gwen's hand and gazed steadily into her eyes. "We know there's something you're not telling us." At Gwen's hurt look she quickly said. "We know you're somehow involved in the missing people. For crying out loud, your own sister is missing! If you're in trouble, you can ask us for help."

"We're your friends." Willie nodded solemnly; "We came here to help you. We never expected to find you mixed up in a missing person problem, but we want to help."

"If you need a lawyer, my cousin works as a paralegal, he can find someone for you." Reba offered. "If you need money…."

Gwen rolled her eyes. "I can't believe this!" She cried. "You think I'm in legal trouble? If you only knew…." Out of the corner of her eye, she caught Colin frowning at her from behind a sculpture of, fittingly enough, a large eye, and closed her mouth. "Um, I'm fine, it's just like I said…. I got a guy who takes care of me. Besides, aren't we supposed to be talking about my sister?"

Willie muttered under his breath. "I thought we were."

The three friends spoke for a long time, and Reba told Gwen what little they knew and what they had been doing to find Emily. At last, they suggested going to a cafe and getting breakfast, but Gwen gave a lame excuse and said she might have some ideas but couldn't tell them much. She shrugged her shoulders and left.

"I can't really believe my best friend is messed up in what for all intents looks like the sex trade! Missing girls all over the city, no one willing to do much, and that includes the cops!"

Willie sighed; "I can't believe it either. But the other option is those pictures and videos from her thumb drive. And THAT can't be true! Vampires aren't real!?"

"They aren't. I'm so confused right now though. Let's get some sleep and try again later."

As they let themselves into the boarding house, Mrs. LaBeof yelled at them from the back of the house. Something about making sure they secured the deadlock and she was tired of having to remind everyone about it.

"Didn't you set the deadlock, Reba?"

"Yeah, I'm sure I did. Landlady's just getting old I guess."

Chapter Twenty

The sky was turning a lesser shade of black when Colin unlocked the door to his mansion and carried Gwen inside. She had lingered too long talking with her friends and had fallen to the curse of the newly made vampire; she had fainted dead [really dead] away, forcing Colin to carry her as he flew through the streets. Her cedar chest was still in the basement, and he gently placed her in it, his hand lingering on her brow. "Why do I put up with you? What is it about you that makes me care for you? I have made others before, what is it about you that is different?" Carefully closing the chest, he leaned against it for several minutes before climbing into his own casket and descending into the slumber of the dead.

The eastern sky faded from black to violet to yellow as the sun rose and traveled its path across the sky. Birds woke and sang their challenges to their rivals. Small breezes stirred the curtains of people unwary enough to leave their windows open at night and late night partiers went back to their hotel rooms to sleep off the indulgence.

Eternal Diet *Wendy Wilson*

Cafe workers donned their aprons and ground the beans to brew the fresh coffee New Orleans loved. This pulled in the first tourists trying to get a jump on the crowds. Before long the tables filled with families enjoying a typical New Orleans breakfast; salmon toast with capers, boudin balls, or a more adventurous catfish with grits along with the more standard fare of eggs and bacon. But why come all the way to New Orleans and not taste its unique cuisine. Waiters and waitresses hurried back and forth taking orders and bringing fresh coffee and juice.

The day wore on as the night's mishaps were discovered and the police called. More names added to the list and more bodies for the coroner. One new patrolman, on seeing the body of a smartly dressed businessman with his throat torn out went deeper into the alley and vomited his donuts and coffee. His partner crouched down and tried to see if the blood surrounding him had viable footprints. Only one, a high heeled women's shoe, was barely visible, so he took a few photos and motioned for the waiting coroner's assistant to take the body. "Not much to find here. Again."

Afternoon ramped up the town's mood, and while families focused on the Aquarium and the Audubon Zoo, the serious partiers started to arrive.

Eternal Diet   Wendy Wilson

Before long the street bands had begun in earnest, and the streets filled with wandering tourists who still couldn't believe [but happily discovering] that it was legal to walk around with alcohol.

The sun began its descent; and the cafes and restaurants switched to their dinner menus and geared up for another night of entertainment and eating. Even the growing number of dead bodies found in the streets wasn't going to stop them from providing for the tourists' every desire. Besides, the bodies were only winos and bums, weren't they? A couple of them were found every morning. So what if the number was increasing, tourism was going strong. Yeah, that had to be it, more tourists so of course more bodies. They kept telling themselves that until they believed it.

In one of the few basements in New Orleans, something that could be referred to as life was stirring. The dark was complete, no glimmer of the lingering sun penetrated the secret room as Colin pushed the cover of his casket away and sat up. He had little difficulty seeing in the pitch. Even if he did, the path to the hidden door was well memorized. Up in the living room, he sat in one of the stuffed armchairs and contemplated the events and his emotions of last night.

Gwen wasn't the first vampire he had 'made.' There had been others. Others he had never felt emotions for, they had all been made when he needed assistance to do his bidding. They had been chosen because of a characteristic he had found necessary to his life at the time. None of them were remembered, let alone mourned when they failed or left to be on their own. So what was different this time?

For a very long time, Colin had not felt any stirring of affection for anyone. He could not understand why Gwen was different, and it bothered him. Emotions were something to be ignored, there was no need for them, and indeed, they were dangerous.

"Penny for your thoughts." Startled, Colin jumped out of his chair and swung around to see Gwen standing in the doorway. She took a quick step back. "Hey, I didn't mean to make you jump, it's just that you looked so lost in thought."

"I was." came the curt reply. "I was thinking of your behavior last night." The startled mien was replaced by one of displeasure. "Do you have any memory of what happened; how you got home safely last night?"

They stood facing each other, one face angry and maybe even a bit embarrassed, the other wondering why he was acting this way.

"No, I'm sorry. I was so caught up with what Reba and Willie were talking about, where they have been looking for Emily and what they've found. They've made some progress." A small smile played on her lips. "They think they know which bars she checked out. And guess what."

"All right. I'll bite."

Gwen paused; did he realize the puns he sometimes made? "One of the bars was the same one the nasty pair tried to abduct me from!"

"Then that is where we will begin tonight's search."

Not so long later the two of them strolled the streets looking for a meal to start the night. Many people thronged the sidewalks, most were just there for the music, and liberal drinking policies and Gwen felt a twinge of guilt. Back when she had idolized vampires and decided to do all she could to become one, she had never really stopped to think fully about the ramifications. Now, watching all these probably good-natured folks enjoying themselves she didn't like to think of making her livelihood by killing them. Was there any other option? Attacking criminals and thieves was one way, but that opened up a problem in itself; it was inherently more dangerous since targets like that were more likely to be aware. And the unaware innocents didn't deserve to die just because she was hungry!

She stopped on a corner, her hunger at war with her dislike of hurting someone. Colin went a few steps and realizing his companion had stopped, turned around and looked quizzically at her.

"What is wrong?"

"Remember when we first met, and I asked you about the type of person you ate from?" A passing tourist overheard her question and grabbed the arm of his partner and hurried out of earshot. Colin frowned at them and pulled Gwen into a quiet corner.

"Yes, I remember. What about it?"

"Back then you said that not all vampires held to drinking from lowlifes. And I see that we follow that rule but…Do we have to kill them?"

Colin threw his hands up in the air. "Now? Now your conscience asserts itself?"

Exasperation flew into her voice. "Well, I'm new to all this! At first, it was exciting, and I just wanted more and more. I couldn't control myself. But now, because of my 'unique metabolism,' I can't eat all I want. And I'm wondering if we have to kill them all." She shrugged. "That's it."

For a moment it looked as if Colin was going to appeal to the heavens again like he had at their first meeting, but he gathered himself. With a slow shake of his head, he answered. "Yes, of course, it is possible to limit your feeding on any one meal. You of all people should be aware of the value of restraint. The question is why would you want to. We are not the judges."

Like a recalcitrant school girl, Gwen kicked her shoe on the pavement. "So, if we can avoid killing why don't more vampires leave their prey alive?"

A mist rose up and swirled around their ankles and was blown away by the opening of the door of the cafe they were standing in front of as the partygoers laughed and called to one another. Colin took Gwen's arm and guided her to a bench far enough away for no random passerby to hear them. When they were settled, he began.

"We can leave them alive. But there is a price, and the victim is the one to pay it. Anytime we drink from a victim and leave them alive, they lose a little of their willpower, and we gain power over them for a period of time, perhaps a day, sometimes longer. A strong-willed person can resist and escape our control, but a weaker one is vulnerable to our will. Enough feedings from one victim results in a virtually brain-dead slave. A slave who willingly provides nourishment for his master."

"But...." Gwen replied.

"But the problem then is these slaves have no thoughts, the master has to tell them to do everything, even down to tie their own shoes. Can you see why that can be cumbersome?"

"I can see where it might be a problem to have to tell someone everything they do, but what if you only eat a small meal from several people?"

"The effect is cumulative." At her look of confusion he sighed heavily, and when he went on, he spoke slowly. "Stronger willed people can shake the effects much better than weaker willed ones, but even so there is a 'build up' so to speak. Do you remember every victim you have had?"

"No, but..." Gwen tried to remember every time she had fed, only a few faces stood out, and that was because she had targeted them specifically. "What does it matter? If you never eat from the same one?"

"Impossible to remember everyone. When you have lived the centuries I have, you will understand. Leaving one alive one time is a chance, but if you return to the same victim, even if it is weeks later, you are beginning the creation of a slave. Now, you might want a slave, but I have never liked having someone in bondage to me although there have been others of our kind who do. I prefer to avoid such vampires."

Gwen realized vampires had to work below the level of awareness and that meant not leaving blithering fools all over the city. Ah well, what it took to learn to be a blood drinker! Would she ever figure it all out? Every time she thought she had it figured out; the explanations would blow it up.

The sight of a human coming out of a bar across from them that seemed to fit the description of an empty willed person grabbed her attention. He, or she, it was hard to tell because his or her posture was slouched, and he was focused more on the concrete walkway than the beautiful sights and sounds floating around. A pair of festive tourists burst out of a door right in front of him, and if not for his partner grabbing his arm and pulling him to the side, he would have bumped right into them.

And that partner! Gwen knew in an instant she was no tourist. She was not tall, but her posture and carriage imbued her with the bearing of a harpy queen ready to swoop on the unlucky. Power radiated from her very skin which was pale as Carrera marble worthy of a Michelangelo sculpture. It took no special powers for Gwen to recognize another of her own kind.

Gwen chanced a look at Colin. Every muscle in his body was tense and still as a statue made of that same marble. He had spotted the newcomer too. "Come, we must leave. Now."

A block away Gwen finally got Colin to stop. "That was one of those slaves we were talking about, wasn't it! And the woman with him was controlling him!"

"Yes, it is exactly what we were discussing. I thought this city clear of them. That's why I came here to get away...."

"Get away?" Gwen almost shouted, but Colin put his finger to her mouth in warning. "You mean you have met these before?"

"I have had dealings with the vampires who enjoy creating slaves. Believe me, you do not want to have any interaction with them."

"I believe you, Colin. But did you see which bar they had come out of?" At his puzzled headshake, she explained. "They came out of the same bar the pair tried to kidnap me from. And there's more." Her voice dropped until only a vampire could hear. "It's the same bar Reba and Willie believe Emily went into looking for me."

Chapter Twenty-One

Emily climbed up two flights of stairs and down a long hallway all in complete darkness after her interview. The red-haired wraith held her with a secure grip. Not sure if it was to guide her or prevent her from running away but where she would run was a mystery, so she pretended he was there to guide her. At the end of the hall, Red stopped and unlocked a door. It swung open, and Emily could see a small but not uncomfortable room much like you would see in a charming bed and breakfast. A miniature boudoir lamp gave off barely enough light for her to see well enough not to bark her shins.

"This is where you will stay until Madame decides what to do with you."

"What do you...." The door shut and the click of the lock made it clear she wouldn't get any answers, let alone an exit. Exhausted and shaking from the last few days Emily curled upon the bed. He mind whirred, and she thought she would never sleep but, with a soft mattress as an unfair advantage, sleep won.

Eternal Diet   Wendy Wilson

When she awoke, she couldn't tell what time it was, couldn't in fact, know if it was day or night. At least her accommodations were better than they had been. There was a real bed with sheets and pillows, and the soft whirr of a machine stirring air towards her spoke of a fan not far off. The tiny light was on, struggling to bring some sort of illumination to the situation. It was still the only source of light in the room. There has got to be a window or something!

She climbed down from the bed, ignoring the morning need we all have, and stepped forward, sliding her toes gingerly towards the lamp. It stood on a small, round table draped with a dark linen cloth. It even had fringes. Reaching out, Emily came up against a wall. No window. So she slid her hand carefully along the contour of the embossed wallpaper. That took her further away from the light source and exposed her to the dangers inherent in any bedroom; a chair blocked her way and knocked her off balance, but she caught herself and found the wall again.

A few feet away from the chair her fingers stubbed against a wooden frame, and in a moment, she discovered it was a doorframe! And the knob turned! It opened into that most necessary of rooms but had no other door or window. A few minutes later, relieved and hands washed she continued her reconnaissance. Another door, this one did not open, and she figured it was the door to the hall. She slid her hand up and down next to the door and hit against a switch. Flipping it on, the room was illuminated in the weak light of a small overhead fixture.

When she finally stopped blinking from even that tiny amount of brightness, Emily took stock of the room. It was about 12x12 with a single bed and small table and chair. There were curtains on the wall she had not yet explored. She threw up the heavy drapes to peer outside. Black. At first, she thought it was the dead of night, but she couldn't even see the lights of other buildings. And if anything, New Orleans was a city that never turned off the lights. Someone had painted over the windows with blackout paint. A few scratches with her nails told her that the paint was on the outside.

The rattle of the doorknob turning and the door swinging open spun her around. Framed within the darker hallway was a small, stooped figure. One of the minions. And it was holding a tray with food. "Is that for me?" Emily put on a cheery smile as the smell of coffee and toast wafted to her. The gray-clad minion shuffled across the room and laid the tray on the small lamp table. It barely balanced and would have fallen in Emily hadn't grabbed it before it toppled. "Hey, can you tell me if it's day outside?" She asked, desperate for any interaction at all. "It's just that it's so dark in here and I can't see out the window. Any idea when they will let me out?" That last bit was spoken to the slumped back of the departing minion. "Ok. Well then, I'll just eat this... Thanks."

It's amazing what a cup of coffee and English muffin can do for the spirits of a scared woman. Before too long, Emily was feeling quite a bit more like herself. Maybe she could get out of here. Her eyes were adjusting to the dark, or was it that some light was making it through the black paint? Either way, she was able to make out more of her surroundings. Which appeared as if it was set dressed for a Victorian romance.

The overwhelming impression was of a dark space lit with the tiny light in the corner table. It was a weak bulb indeed, probably no more than a few candles worth of illumination. By focusing her eyes away from the light they gradually were able to make out more details. The wallpaper was dark flocking over slightly lighter shade smooth. There was carpets, which upon close examination revealed a lovely pattern of vines and roses were interwoven across its length. The curtains were weighty and embroidered with heavy brocade. And the fringe! Everywhere

Eternal Diet *Wendy Wilson*

fringe! Fringe on the rug, fringe on the curtains, fringe on the blanket, fringe on the pillow case and fringe on the fabric laying over the lamp!

Unlike most Victorian rooms, it was not full of clutter but stood rather stark in comparison. No large collection of painting and pictures on the wall or dozens of knick-knacks littered shelves. She could see only one bed, table and chair, and the bathroom door. And she could see even clearer that there was no way she could get out.

Chapter Twenty-Two

"Are you sure? Absolutely sure this is the bar?"

"I know it was the one we lured those nasty couples from." It dawned on Gwen. "You know this bar, don't you? It wasn't news to you that the bar had a reputation, was it? Ooooh, I could hit you!"

"Why? It was good practice for you, and at the time we didn't know your sister was coming here or that she would find herself entangled with the owners of the bar. And for your information, I only knew of people going missing, not that it was connected in any way to others of our kind. We are not the only cause of pretty women going missing you know. Come, you are hungry and letting your anger blind you to your need."

The two of them strolled along the avenues. Full dark and the fog in the less-traveled areas made them almost disappear into the shadows, and before long they came up behind a furtive-looking fellow who was glancing around him as if he didn't want to be seen.

Eternal Diet *Wendy Wilson*

Colin put his hand on Gwen's arm, but she had already spotted the suspicious actor. "There's a prime candidate for 'evildoer' for dinner" he whispered. "Let's see just what he has in mind."

"I can't wait Colin. I'm hungry." He lifted his hands to let her go, and she almost sprang away. But at just that moment the lurker crouched and slid behind a doorway and flattened himself against a wall, so she stopped herself before the run.

A pair of women, one in slacks and the other in a too tight dress who were not being as careful as they should have been, walked past the doorway, gossiping about the handsome guys they had flirted with. They probably thought the buddy system would keep them safe. They were wrong.

The mugger snuck up behind them and hit slacks girl as the other lit a cigarette. She fell without a sound. Too tight dress turned to where her partner should have been to offer her a hit and when her friend wasn't there, she whirled around just in time to get a fist in her face, and she went down too as the mugger started rifling through their belongings.

"I've seen enough" Gwen growled, and in an instant, she had the man by his throat. "Picking on innocent women, are we? Not when I'm hungry!" He gurgled in panic, and when he saw her eyes gleaming with vampiric brightness, he panicked and started kicking and flailing about. "Ah, a lively one tonight! Just what I need to get my blood going!" The mugger's last sentient thoughts were 'why is she laughing about getting blood going?' Gwen carried her still jerking dinner into the alleyway a few doors down and licked her teeth. Nice and sharp.

Positioning him so his throat was best exposed she knelt beside him and slowly licked his face. His eyes, already bugging out of their sockets rolled back, and a strangled scream came from his lips. "No, no no, little man. No noise, please. It is rude to interrupt a meal with noise." Gwen giggled. "Have you no manners? No? I take your silence as a no."

She placed her hand over his mouth and said "Shhhh, this won't hurt a bit. Well, not me at least." As her teeth sunk into the jugular warm, salty blood sprayed into her mouth. A most pleasurable sensation threading from nipples to groin made her pause for a moment and groan with pleasure. She held her breath to prolong the feeling. Her nipples hardened as she released long enough to arch her back and enjoy the sudden clamping and a sudden wetness spread between her legs. Her toes curled, and for a second the world stopped.

Eternal Diet — Wendy Wilson

Her concentration broken, the meal feebly wriggled, slamming her back to reality. Gwen bent down and resumed drinking. With his heart beating in terror the blood pumped faster than she could swallow and dribbled down her chin onto the meal's shirt. Finally, his heart slowed. It started skipping, and Gwen pulled out. Giving a tiny bite to her tongue, she ran the trickle of blood from it over the puncture marks and looked on approvingly as they closed, leaving no indication of any wound. She stood up and walked back onto the street where Colin was standing over the still inert girls.

"You didn't feed from them, did you? They're innocents!"

"Not as innocent as you might think but no, I did not feed from them." At her puzzled look, he explained. "I do not need to feed every night. As you get older, you won't either. Some of the oldest ones only feed several times a year and then it isn't always because they need to."

Gwen shrugged. "Learn something new every day, er, night."

He looked at her. "That meal took you long enough. You normally don't 'relish' it quite that much."

Gwen rolled her eyes. "Like I said, I was hungry. And not just for food."

Mealtime dealt with, they started walking towards the now suspect bar. It was not all that late and since it was never late in New Orleans, they had to weave their way through the crowds until they arrived. Now, this bar wasn't one of the 'bright' lights of New Orleans. It was on one of the lower quarter side streets. It did its best to mimic the other, more famous bars by using a pirate theme and a drink suspiciously close in name to a much more famous pirate-themed club, but the pure fact was, this bar was dark and small and off the beaten track. What it lacked in a tourist attraction, it made up in cheap drink prices, so it did draw a crowd on busy nights. And as in pretty much every bar worthy of the name in New Orleans had live entertainment, so did this one.

On stage was a trio of what looked like high school kids playing in a garage band. But their music… now that was different. These kids knew how to play. Colin and Gwen chose a table in a corner but close enough to see what was happening at the bar and, more importantly, the door behind the bar. A waitress approached and took their order of mixed drinks and left. "What are we gonna do with the drinks? We can't really drink them!"

Eternal Diet   *Wendy Wilson*

Colin raised an eyebrow. "Why do you think I chose this table? See the potted plant right next to us? Figure it out."

"Well, you don't have to be smug about it. I'm new to this." Gwen complained. "For all I know we can drink alcohol, and you never told me!"

"We can't. But we can pretend." Colin smiled up to the waitress and paid for the drinks and laid a nice tip on the tray. "We have some business to discuss and don't need anything to eat. But thank you."

"No problem sir. My name is Amelia and if you need anything, just let me know." She pocketed the more than generous tip into her apron pocket and went on with her job.

For the next few hours, the two of them sat at the table, occasionally surreptitiously dumping the drinks and ordering new ones. But mostly they watched the bar and the door behind it. Not much happened until they were on their third drink. Gwen was trying to decide if she should start acting a bit drunk to keep up the pretense when Colin tapped her forearm with his finger and pointed. "Look at the doorway." Gwen turned her head the little bit needed to see behind the bar and there she was. "That's the one we saw with the slavey!"

The lady in question was talking to the bartender. He was nodding and indicating a pair of pretty tourists who were clearly beyond their drink level. The woman shook her head no.

"Probably too high profile. They likely have family who will miss them right away. These monsters don't want to deal with the heat that stealing pretty tourists will bring." Colin's voice dropped a level. "Look what happened with your sister. They know that people are looking for her." Gwen gulped a little. Her sister! Her sister was in the hands of these monsters! A sudden realization hit her; SHE was one of those 'monsters'!

Colin's hand gripped Gwen's, and his impassioned tone brought her back. "We are not monsters. We feed on blood, but we do not imprison and enslave our prey. We do not reduce the population around us to soulless poverty and despair! We are better. We are honorable." His voice rose to a clearly audible level at the last sentence and several drinkers twisted around to see who was talking about 'honor' and 'being better.'

Gwen stood up, dragging Colin with her. "Ha! He's had too much to drink, folks! Sorry. Better get him back to the hotel." With that, she and Colin left the bar. Both bartender and woman ignored them and kept scanning the room.

"Now, do you mind telling me what that was all about? Any louder and our cover would've been blown!"

"I am sorry, Gwen. But I have had dealings with vampires like them, and it twists my soul to think of it. I was, at one time, a part of them. My 'maker' was one of the leaders. A long time ago. In another country." Gwen could only look at him in shock.

"You mean… you were…That's why you know so much about them and their methods! Oh my god! Why didn't you tell me earlier?"

"Because of exactly that reason! I can't control the anger I feel against them. I want to rip and tear them apart and lap up their blood from the dirt."

"Ok, I think I understand. What are we going to do now?"

"You can never understand, but for now you will stay here and continue watching the bar."

"Me? What about you? Where are you going?" "I am going to feed. I feel the need for blood." He turned and was gone. Gwen sat on a stone bench and settled in for a long vigil.

Chapter Twenty-Three

A few minutes of super-fast walking brought Colin into an area of town not much frequented by tourists. In fact, tourists were advised to stay away from this area at night. That's why Colin went there.

Within moments the reason for his choosing this part of town appeared. A mean looking creep was fast stepping down the almost abandoned street dragging a small child with him. The child looked to be no more than 10 years old for all that her makeup and high heels tried to make her look older. She was pulling away for all she was worth, but the bully jerked her hard until she stumbled into a trot to keep from being dragged on the sidewalk. "C'mon you little whore, yer mama said I could have you. And I paid good money for you!" He growled at the girl's cries. "And quit yer hollering! It ain't as if you didn't know this was coming."

Colin watched closely as the man went into the lobby of a cheap boarding house. He stopped outside of one of the rooms and fumbled with his keys while the girl cowered in the doorway between his legs.

Eternal Diet — *Wendy Wilson*

Tears ruined the overdone mascara and rouge and she looked younger than her earlier 10 years estimate. "Please don't, mister. I never did this before! I never even had my monthlies!"

Lust thickened the man's throat. "That's why I paid more, you little whore. I get to be the one that pops you." The girl wailed and bully hit her, sending her against the jam of the now open door. "I told you…." His voice suddenly turned to a gargle. His eyes popped out as he stared down into the blood red eyes of a very, very angry vampire who had lifted him up by his throat.

Colin looked down at the little girl and said. "I don't think you want to watch this." He threw the man into the dingy room and followed him in.

The girl couldn't run, her knees refused to let her stand. She scooted a few feet back and covered her head. She couldn't see what was happening, but she could hear it well enough. At first there was a lot of furniture breaking noises and yells of fury from an inhuman throat that froze her blood. Then cries of "Mercy! And "Help!"" from the would be rapist. Those cries she almost enjoyed. She knew well there would be no help for him in this neighborhood.

Very quickly his cries turned from cries for help to screams of pain to howls of pure terror. And then soft things started being thrown around the room. Some of them landed in a soft plop of a mix of liquid and something a bit firmer. She opened her fingers and ventured a peek.

The door was open a foot or so and from her vantage point of the hallway she could see what looked like the bully's hand and part of his arm. It was the end not attached to the hand that froze her; it was ragged with blood pulsing from it. A glint of white of a bone, twisted and splintered stuck out as if reaching for the rest of the arm.

The cries and howls stopped, to be replaced by the sound of someone, something drinking. Then the someone or something stood up and slowly walked to the door. The girl crouched rooted, unable to tear her eyes from the arm in the doorway, her bruised face and thin body unable to move. She was so terrified of the man standing before her she wet her pants.

"Did your mother truly sell you to him?" His voice held vestiges of the roars she had heard but his tone was gentle. He followed her gaze and saw the arm remnant. "You will never have to worry about him again." His gentle voice released her fear and she collapsed into tears.

"Wh, wha, what did you do to him?"

"I stopped him from ever hurting anyone ever again."

She ventured a look at his face. No trace of anger or blood or violence remained on it. His eyes were not the blood red she had glimpsed as he clenched the rapist's throat. He had gone from terror to protector and she accepted that much like she had already accepted her life was never going to be easy. "Wh...What happens now?"

"Now we get your mother to answer for her deeds." He held out his hand to her and she took it. "Come, where do you live?" As she walked past the now open doorway, she risked a glance. Blood was splattered all over the walls, ceilings and floor. On the floor were lumps of 'something' resembling the steaks her mom sometimes got when her clients paid well. Only these lumps were darker, with much fresher blood. Some were long with bone sticking out but mostly they were pretty shapeless. A few had remnants of clothing wrapped around them.

In a corner on what used to be a chair she could make out hair the color of the rapists. It was attached to something white and shaped something like a round ball with two holes in the front. Blood dripped down from that too and joined with the blood from the lumps. The little girl with the bruised face and ruined

Eternal Diet *Wendy Wilson*

make up looked up at Colin. "What will you do to my mommy?"

"Make sure she never hurts you again too."

Chapter Twenty-Four

Gwen sat on the stone bench watching the doorway of the bar. The usual back and forth of tourists and locals out for a good time. With so many excellent choices for entertainment in New Orleans, no one place, unless it was run by a famous celebrity, seemed to get more business than the others. Partygoers would drift back and forth between establishments, usually starting out with the expensive places but, as the night wore on and their wallets wore down, more of them started looking for the cheaper places. Like the place Gwen watched so keenly.

Business was definitely picking up for it. Gwen watched as a group of definite touristy types stopped outside of 'her' bar. There seemed to be an argument about something. Of the five, four appeared to want to leave, but one holdout, a pretty girl in shorts and a tank top, insisted rather loudly that the night was too young. Her hair was in a bouncy streaked blond ponytail on top of her tall, slim and athletic body. It was clear she was wearing flats, not because they were more comfortable but because all the males in the group were on the short side. She had a tan so perfect it had to have come from a bottle and tanning bed, and her perky boobs owed none of their lifting power to artificial means; internal or external. This was a woman who knew what the gym was for...getting laid.

Even with her enhanced hearing, Gwen could only make out a small portion of what was said but when the tank top girl slurred "Fi... fine, you ga home. I'm gonna st... *hic* stay!" Her instincts engaged and she narrowed in on the girl. Who, rather comically, managed to turn her drunken spin into a drunken gravitas walk to step up into the dark building.

Just the type for those in the bar to take a special interest in. Her friends would probably not even remember the name of the street, let alone the name of the bar and Miss Pony Tail would probably not remember anything at all. Gwen twisted around on the bench hoping to see Colin, but all that was there were more partiers plying the sidewalk. "Damn, Colin! Hurry on back. I think things are gonna go down soon."

Sure enough, about a half hour after Miss Pony Tail went into the bar, one of the slaveys stepped out onto the sidewalk and disappeared into the dark. Soon after, the bartender's companion opened the door and also disappeared into the darkness. The difference between the two leave-takings was that the second one included an even more drunk, or possibly drugged, Miss Pony Tail. A late model four-door sedan swung up alongside them and opened its door allowing the two women to climb in. "Well, I better get on with it." Gwen decided. "Colin will just have to deal with me gone." And she followed behind the car, which was fortunately not hurtling through the late night crowds still wandering the streets but was heading deep into the swamp.

It took all of Gwen's attention to stay close enough to the car to see where it turned but at the same time far enough away so that someone with the abilities of a vampire would not suspect it was being followed. The car finally turned into the driveway of a once fine home. Gravel crunched as the tires rolled up to the far side of the house.

A slam and then another slam and then footsteps, one pair carefully placing onto the paving stones of a walkway and the other dragging and stumbling. "Take the car to the garage, I won't be needing you anymore tonight. I do believe Madame will be pleased with my prize." The car backed up and turned around, its headlights shining right at the bush Gwen crouched behind. She ducked into a thicker section and held her breath. But apparently, the sexy vampire was too happy with her catch to catch anything else.

"Now, my pretty little drunken girl, we shall let you sleep off your indulgence and tomorrow night I will introduce you to Madame. And she will decide what to do with you." It sounded like they were descending a short stair as her voice slowly sounded further away.

"Yesh….sleep, zhank you…I musta had a little too mush!" Miss Ponytail giggled and stumbled along into the building.

Her companion chuckled an ominous laugh. "Oh yes indeed. A bit of sleep and you'll never feel better."

Gwen couldn't resist doing a little fist pump of victory but the only "YES!" she allowed herself was in her head. We've got 'em! I know where they live! But… before I go back and find Colin I'm going to do a little bit of reconnaissance and see what we have here. Hope started to rise in her that this was where Emily was. It was the same bar Reba and Willie thought Emily had checked out. And a woman had just been kidnapped from it. It sounded too much alike to be a coincidence. She looked down at her fancy shoes and pretty but confining dress. "Can't poke around with this get-up."

Eternal Diet   *Wendy Wilson*

A few minutes later a barefooted Gwen with her tight dress slit up the side slunk around the corner of the building. One careful circuit of the ground level revealed no windows and the only doors were sure to be guarded. A strange but eerily familiar scent drifted into the air. Gwen sniffed. Sure she should be able to identify it, she closed her eyes and let it wash over her. A feeling unpleasant and disturbing tickled in the back of her mind.

Just underneath the floral scent of the blossoms, there was the wisp of decay, like meat left on the counter a bit too long. Finally, she realized why the smell was familiar.... It smelled like her coffin, like Colin's coffin. It smelled like vampire. A lot of vampires. Gwen's breath stopped. For the smell to be that strong there had to be a veritable coven of vampires. Not just the few she and Colin had suspected. What had they done to Emily? She was part way up the side of the brick before she realized it. Whoa! Yet another thing vampires can do Colin never told me about! We can climb walls!

Very carefully, because she didn't know just how close to the wall the vampires on the other side were and if they could sense her through it, she slowly inched herself up to a second story window. It was painted black. Figures. No light in that way. I'm gonna have to give up for now and come back with Colin.

A small sob from just above her caught her attention. It couldn't be the drunken girl, she was probably passed out. Who then? Hope rose higher as she climbed to the windowsill. The sobbing continued, low and with an underpinning of anger. "I am so going to make them pay for this!" Gwen almost lost her grip. It was Emily's voice! And it was coming from inside the room.

If only she could see her! She couldn't knock on the window; that would alert the other inhabitants of the house. Her hands pressed against the window her fingers clenching reflexively. A flake of black paint chipped off and stuck to her fingernail. She scraped a little more, this time in the bottom corner.

Emily's sobbing stopped, and the sound of someone climbing off a bed encouraged her to scrape more. Finally a small spot just large enough for an eyeball was left. A green iris with brown flecks filled the spot. The eye spun left and right as well as up and down until it spotted Gwen's pale face. Gwen smiled and called. "Emily!" Then all hell broke loose.

Emily's eye was jerked away from the peephole, and another took its place. This one was not human. A large black pupil within a pale blue iris rimmed with

Eternal Diet   *Wendy Wilson*

blood red lids glared angrily out. A roar through the window unfroze Gwen, and she dropped to the ground and sped away into the night as roars of fury echoed behind her. Howls of outrage bellowed out in her wake. She did not hear the commanding voice that called back her pursuers. "Let her go. Our bait has caught something."

Chapter Twenty-Five

Earlier in the evening as Gwen and Colin were pretending to drink in the bar, Emily dozed in her dark room. Without sunlight to indicate the passage of day or night, it was difficult to tell what part of the day it was, and she had fallen into the doze, wake, doze cycle that happens with people unable to attend to the passage of time. She couldn't judge if she had been there hours or even days.

There had only been that one meal, and though it was of better quality than the meals in the cell, it had not really satisfied her hunger, and her stomach was making its protests known. The growling told her it had been probably close to at least a full day. At least she had all the water she wanted.

As her head nodded and her eyes closed for that knew the amount of times, the sudden twisting of the doorknob jerked her head up. Yes! Someone was opening the door. Was it dinner? Or something far worse? Emily held her breath and watched as the door swung open to reveal the red-haired creature who had escorted her to the room. He stared unblinkingly at the frightened woman curled up with her arms clutching around her legs on the bed. Red-rimmed eyes bore into Emily's.

A faint smile played on its lips. "You are to come with me."

"Why?" The smile vanished.

"You are to come with me, now."

"I'm hungry, can I have something to eat?" Another smile, this one showing brilliantly white teeth just a little too ragged for comfort.

"Oh, don't fear. There will be feeding." And he motioned her into the hall.

This time her guide took her into a different room. Not quite as large as the throne like room from before; it was smaller and more intimate. And Emily did not hear the sheer volume of whispering and rustling as from her first time. There was even a little more light, only the furthest corners were in complete darkness and what whispering she heard came from those dark voids.

"I hope you appreciate my efforts to make you more comfortable, my dear." Emily recognized the voice at once as the ancient matriarch from before. "I have directed my staff to not tease you. They do love teasing my visitors!" Short, wheezing sounds came from the same corner as the voice, sounding as if someone was trying to start a mower by pulling the rope too quickly. It took a moment, but Emily realized it was laughter.

It stopped, and an entirely new sense of tension filled the room. "Enough fun and games. It is time for a real conversation. Come closer. I promise not to bite." The mower tried to start again, and Emily gulped, glad now that her meal had been so small.

The closer she came to the tiny woman perched on the only chair in the room, the deeper Emily's feeling of wrongness grew. There was something wrong, very wrong with this woman. Wrong with her face, wrong with her hands and impossibly long nails, wrong with her voice and everything wrong in the way she didn't blink as Emily approached. The woman sat perfectly still, her coal black eyes penetrating into Emily. No movement, no breath. Nothing to say she was alive. Except for the eyes. From the depths came a flickering light, a burning deep down that glowed and beckoned Emily closer like a cobra poised and ready to strike.

"Yess, that's good. Come closer." The room fell completely silent, no whispers, no rustling. The very air went still. Emily tried but couldn't break the stare, couldn't command her own eyes to turn away. Black eyes getting closer and closer boring into Emily's soul like a mouse before the serpent. Closer until that was all she could see, the black encompassed all of the universe. She wanted to fall into those eyes. She wanted to scream and claw at the eyes. She could do neither. The room darkened, and her vision narrowed to the tiny pinpricks of light boring into her soul.

Her heart started beating louder and louder and faster and faster until it felt like it was going to tear out of her chest into the hands of the woman in front of her. Madame smiled a cheerless smile and broke the stare to look longingly at Emily's pulsing veins. Her lips parted, and her tongue poked out, dampening her top lip. It withdrew, and the smile went with it as she released Emily from her gaze. "Not time for that. Not now. Soon enough."

Madame sat back against the seat's upholstery and considered the quivering female before her. "I don't suppose you know what you have gotten yourself into, do you? Have you any concept of what surrounds you? And why I might be indulging you by letting you live?"

"Letting me live? I just wanted to find my sister?" Emily cried. "Why would you want to kill me? I haven't done anything. If I got to close to your racket, I'm sorry. But I haven't seen anything. Really! You can let me go. I won't be able to tell the cops anything. You don't have to kill me. Please."

"You truly are a foolish girl. Racket?" She looked around in confusion. "What does she mean by 'racket'?" Red appeared beside her and whispered in her ear. She laughed the lawn mower again. "Oh, my dear. We are not engaged in any criminal activity." She paused for a second. "Well, at least not anything as mundane as what you probably think! You see, dumpling."

Another effort to start the lawnmower. "You see, we are something very ancient. We are something that has all but fled from your modern conscience. We are blood drinkers. And so is your sister."

"What did you say?" Emily whispered.

"You heard me, my dear. You know what we are and what your sister has become.

"That's impossible! You're lying! I don't believe you!" In the back of her mind, Emily had to accept what the ancient woman had said. She and Reba and Willie had seen too many unexplainable things. Inexplicable except for the one explanation they had all danced around. Outrageous as it sounded as the axiom went; when you have stripped away all that is possible, then all that is left, however improbable is the truth. And yes, as impossible as it sounded, it was probable that vampires did exist and… No, she couldn't say it, couldn't even think it!

Emily's legs shook and held her upright no more. She fell to her knees. "It can't be. Liar!" Her shoulders shook. Her hands clenched tightly. Later she would find little crescents of blood where her nails had cut her palms. Fear and anger and desperation waged within her. The shadows around the room threatened to swoop in, but with a tiny movement of her exquisitely manicured hand, Madame motioned to let Emily continue. Her eyes and lips narrowed as she watched the woman sobbing on the floor. "All I wanted was to find my sister! Why are you doing this?"

Her whole concept of the world was being torn apart. Surely this was some sort of nightmare! It couldn't be real. It certainly couldn't be true! Vampires were the stuff of movies and fantasy novels. They were escapism explanations to the strange things that happened. That's what this had to be! Slowly Emily' sobs reduced to hiccups. Her hands unclenched, and she raised her head to look at Madame. "I don't know why you are doing this, and I really don't care. Let me go. I promise I won't tell anyone."

"I tell you your sister is a blood drinker and you try to bargain with me?" Amazement and a touch of rage ran through Madame's voice. "I can see there is only one way to convince you. And it is what I should have done nights ago." She stood up and advanced towards Emily. Tiny as she was, she loomed and seemed to fill the entire room with her essence. Again Emily felt like a mouse in front of a snake, unable to move a muscle to save itself.

Bloody eyes came closer, grew larger and filled with desire. The cobra's mouth opened, and Emily could see two very sharp teeth. Closer the teeth came. Emily tried to move. Nothing worked. Her legs were like two logs, and her arms merely sticks to hold her from the floor. A stench of fetid air blew at her. She stared at the coming doom and tried to close her eyes.

Suddenly the door flew open, and the woman from the bar came in, dragging Ponytail girl. "Madame! I have news! And we must hurry, I think we were followed!"

Madame drew back. "You are sure you were followed? By who?"

"I'm not sure who she is, but she was with that Scottish blood drinker you asked us to watch out for months ago. They were in the bar watching us. I took this one." She threw the blonde onto the floor. "I took her to tempt them, but I think it is only a female that followed."

Eternal Diet   *Wendy Wilson*

"If they were together in the bar then they must surely be working together."

Madame gestured to Emily. "Take her back to her room for now. If there is an intruder, then there is no time for pleasure right now. Everyone get ready. We have a visitor! "She laughed her lawnmower starter and flew from the room. Shadows from the corners followed her out the door flying to other corners in the house.

Bar lady and Ponytail girl were left. "Where did everyone go? They went so fast!" Ponytail girl giggled, still a bit drunk. "They juss disappeared like that!" She tried to click her fingers together, but sadly, her fingers would not cooperate.

"Oh, shut up, stupid girl. I don't have time to feed right now but remember this: I am hungry." That shut the drunk up.

Red took Emily by the arm and escorted her back to the little dark room where she sat on the bed crying. Rage, fear, sorrow, and outrage flooded her as she sobbed and rocked back and forth, "I'll make them pay for this." Outside her room, it had gone quiet. Dead quiet. She could feel the silence press on her ears, not even the sound of an insect broke the silence. Then a faint sound intruded. It came from the direction of the window. Yes! There is was again! It was coming from the window.

This time it was followed by a scraping noise like nails scratching at a mirror. Was it the intruder, the ancient crone, was both frightened and excited about? How was that possible? Emily knew she had gone up at least two flights of stairs, so that would mean someone had to have climbed at least 20 feet up the outside wall. She got off the bed and tiptoed to the window. Most definitely someone was peeling the paint off, there was a tiny spot in the bottom corner, and she could see movement through. Quickly she put her eye against the hole. A pale, thin but familiar face broke into a smile. It was Gwen! "Gwen!" she yelled. And then all hell broke loose.

Chapter Twenty-Six

Far in the distance, Willie could sense an unnatural presence coming closer. A tiny woman with even tinier feet approached. The air around her shimmered, and the fetid miasma of decay surrounded him, choking his throat. The woman came closer, closer; she was looking for someone or something, asking a question Willie felt he had the answer to. He couldn't see anything. Everywhere darkness and a dead silence ruled. Terror filled his body, and he was unable to move his legs or get away from the agonizing fear that if the woman saw him, he was doomed.

Closer she came. Willie could feel her eyes roaming the dark, searching through the stygian darkness, her own senses growing stronger as she neared his hiding place. He could sense more the closer she came; she was not walking, she floated as if on a draft of air. Her face became better defined; it was ageless and ancient, lined with wrinkles yet flushed with the dewiness of youth. The lips did not move as she spoke; Come to me and live forever, come to me and fight my foes beside me!

Willie cowered, covered his head with his arms, screwed his eyes tightly shut and fought to resist the urge to burst forth and offer himself to her will. For he knew it would be the end of him. Quietly chanting the words from a childhood prayer Now, I lay me down to sleep… Willie managed to keep his sanity.

The force of the woman's will receded, and Willie slowly untangled his limbs and opened his eyes. Darkness was all around, even the fetid smell was undiminished, but he could no longer sense the evil presence of the tiny woman. His breath coming in ragged gasps he stood up and tried to look into the darkness. A hint of air stirred against his right ear. He turned to see the horror of the woman's grimacing visage inches away from his face. She screamed "I SEE YOU!!!

Willie jerked awake, his lung laboring, his heart pounding and sweat pouring from his body. He sat there, gasping for control. His mind fought him, and for a while his terror kept him glued to the little cot just like he was glued in the dream. Slowly he regained control, and his heart and lungs slowed from fight or flight to simply scared mode.

He looked at Reba asleep in the bed on the other side of the room. Do I wake her? Or wait. I'm not even sure what the fuck that was or how to even begin to tell her. I'll wait. And he fell back into the pillows only to toss and turn for what seemed an eternity until he finally fell into an uneasy sleep.

Even with the alarm set to wake them at a realistic hour, both of them slept through and didn't wake up until the heat in the room had risen to an unbearable level. "Ugh!" Reba kicked the sheets off her legs. "How does anyone live in this heat? What did they do before air conditioning?"

Willie merely moaned and turned over to look at her. "We forgot to turn on the fan. Yuck. My mouth feels like a baboon took a sand bath in it." He got up and stumbled over to the window. The whir of the fan kicked in, and he stood fully in the flow, lifting his arms and turning around to cool his sweaty body. His dream hit him, and his stomach felt sick. "Reba, I gotta tell you something."

"Well, do it after I take a shower because I can't stand myself."

It was well into the afternoon before they were showered and dressed and ready to brave the outdoor heat of New Orleans. Where to start, where to start. A growl from Willie's stomach answered that question, and they set off to find something to eat. Which, in New Orleans was not difficult at all. A few blocks away was a local favorite shop for a Po-Boy. "Is your stomach up for one of those or do ya want something a bit lighter?" Willie scoffed.

"Did you just hear my stomach? I'm up for a Po-Boy." So, Po-Boy it was.

It took a few minutes to get a seat, and when the waitress came over to their booth with a menu, they waved it aside. Reba took point. "A Po-Boy for both of us."

"Do y'all want it dressed?" asked the waitress. At their obvious confusion, she laughed. "Dressed means all the fixin's honey. And our fixin's are the best if I do say so myself."

"Dress 'em on up then. And what's good to drink with them? We're not looking for beer, but we'll rely on your recommendation for liquid libation thank you." Willie was enjoying the give and take, turning on his charm and smiling at their waitress.

"Ok, two Po-Boys, dressed and two root beers. Be right back with your drinks." She winked at Willie and walked back to the counter.

Reba groaned. "Willie, I can't take you anywhere!"

"What?" He spread his hands in the universal gesture of a palms up shrug. "Is it wrong to smile at a hard-working lady?"

Eternal Diet   *Wendy Wilson*

"A smile is one thing, but you know you'll never act on it. Anyway. Not important. Here come the sodas." The next minute or so was filled with them banging the straws on the table and blowing the paper sleeve at one another. Giggles.

"We gotta get serious, Reba. It feels funny to tell you this in the bright sunshine and daylight, but I had the scariest and most realistic dream last night. It's hard to put into words but let me try.

"Last night I dreamed I was in a dark place with the most horrible smell. It was ugly and stunk like what you'd expect a mass graves would smell like. A woman I'd never seen before was looking for something in the darkness, and she sensed me. And let me tell ya, Reba, it terrified me. She wanted me, or whatever, to come to her for eternal life."

At Reba's widened eyes he went on. "Yeah, eternal life. What are the odds that we suspect, of all unbelievable things, vampires, and then I would have a dream of them so vivid I could SMELL it? Do you know anyone who can smell something during a dream? Other than Gwen that is.

"It gets worse. This woman kept getting closer and closer to me until I was a quivering blob on the floor. And then her presence went away. The stench was still there but not her voice. I got up and looked around. That's when she exploded into my face and screamed: "I see you!"

Reba's worried face reassured Willie she was taking this seriously and wasn't ready to pooh-pooh the idea. That alone scared him a little. The idea that maybe, just maybe; vampires were real turned his world on edge. It was one thing to believe in things beyond our sight, and to have a trusted, down to earth friend believe you. It was quite another for something that belonged to mythology to be walking the earth not far from him. Even worse was it seemed to be aware of HIM. "I was thinking it might be time to go home. But the dream changed it for me, and before we go, I want to check out that bar we think she went to."

Their sandwiches arrived, and they spent the next 20 minutes groaning with delight as they devoured their excellent Po-Boys and sipped their Barq's root beer. The sandwiches were superbly flavored, and they stuffed themselves into a food coma and leaned back into the bench back and smiled benignly. "That was one good sandwich. Almost worth moving to New Orleans for just that."

"Oh, I don't know about almost, Willie! Dare we have a cup of coffee? We're gonna be up late again tonight I bet."

It was late enough for the early bar hoppers, so they took up residence on the bench across from the suspect establishment as it opened its doors for the afternoon traffic. "Tell me again, Willie, about the dream. I'm having trouble accepting this whole thing. Vampires? How can that be?"

"I know it sounds fantastical but think about all we've learned. All the missing people, Gwen's photos and that video. And don't forget those police reports mention a great loss of blood in the victim but no sign of blood where the body is found even though evidence shows that's where they died. The word 'exsanguination' is used quite a lot in those reports. That means…"

"I know what it means. You don't have to spell it out for me. It's just that there's something I didn't tell you before and it has to do with your dream."

Willie looked puzzled. "My dream? What about it? I told you everything I can remember."

Reba hesitated a moment and decided to launch. "Your dream is almost exactly like a dream Gwen told me about. No, don't get upset, let me go on. Before, when we were still in Winchester, you remember she was always trying to lose weight, right?" At Willie's nod, she continued. "I told her about a hypnotist who specialized in changing people's life habits like dieting and smoking and what not. She went. The next day I asked her how it went, and she said she had had the strangest dream about someone coming into her room. She mentioned the smell. That's what got me about your dream, the smell of decay. Only her dream didn't terrify her. It was pleasant she said, almost sexual. That's when she dove into the vampire stuff."

Willie nodded, "Yeah, she got all into that research about mythology having a basis in reality. But I never took it seriously. Did you?"

"Not then. But I am beginning to wonder now. Your dream was not a nice one, but do you think it might be because we are threatening a vampire's domain? Gwen did say her research indicated hypnosis could trigger a sixth sense and maybe turned her infatuation into a passion and then into what we thought was an obsession."

The two of them sat in silence as they realized they were talking about vampires and Gwen as if it were an accepted reality; actually wondering if a vampire was threatened by their search.

Reba reached into her bag and brought out a couple of typewritten pages. "I guess this is as good a time as any to go over this. Did you see this when we were looking for stuff at the room?" Willie nodded.

Eternal Diet — *Wendy Wilson*

"I saw the file listed on the thumb drive, but I didn't see it printed. And then we got distracted, and I never got a chance to read it through. It's about vampires, right?"

"Yep, it is. Gwen was good at research, and she must have been real busy for a while with looking into vampires. I printed it out the other night after we saw Gwen for the first time." She handed Willie the papers and lit a cigarette. "Go on, read'em now. I have a feeling we should know more about these things." Willie began reading.

April 13

Vampires are real. They have been around for millennia, and one theorist believes they began in Egypt as a result of a demon infesting a body after a sorcerer cast a magic spell. Some theorists believe vampires in different parts of the world were begun as a result of a virus that entered a human's bloodstream. Which one is the right one, no one can say, but I think the whole thing began as a virus. Much like the zombie outbreaks in movies.

At least it has more scientific reasoning, and viruses can mutate and do strange things. One thing is for sure; all cultures of the world have stories of blood drinkers in their histories. Vampires are universal and have been around forever.

There are the 'traditional' vampires like Dracula that everyone is familiar with. China has the Jiangshi which goes around consuming the chi of unsuspecting victims. Estries are vampires from Jewish culture. They resemble succubus, but instead of stealing breath, they drink blood. Philippines has the Manananggal.

You name a country or region, and it has a bloodsucking vampire-like creature in its stories. In short, my decision to hunt for a vampire is not deranged. In fact, it is based on much research and investigation.

Willie looks up from his reading. "Ok, so we know she really believed in vampires, and she has a lot of data to back her up. What I want to know is what happened to her? Why did she disappear?"

"Keep reading" was all Reba would say, her voice low and serious.

April 15

It doesn't really matter what type of vampire or where it came from. The ones I am following here in New Orleans most definitely drink blood very neatly. I've seen the newspapers accounts of 'nearly bloodless' drained bodies being found. So that confirms my suspicion that there is at least one, most likely more, vampires operating in New Orleans. The books were right. I'm going out tonight to look again. There is one particular subject I think I have seen a bunch of times.

April 26

There are so many theories on vampires it is hard to pin them down. Do they only feed on evildoers, do they have to have the soil of their land in their coffin, can their reflection be seen in a mirror, do they shapeshift? The list is practically endless, and there are convincing arguments for all of them. The ability I am interested in is the one that brought me here; they are beautiful, and they can grant beauty to someone.

My search is showing results. My friends think I am nuts. Maybe I am. But I am getting very close to something not explainable. Just a few more searches. I can sense one very close at times.

May 4

Oh my god! That's all I can say....My hands are shaking. I've done it! I made contact. And YES, it's the one I thought I saw. I can't believe I did it. Let me take a breath. Calm down. His name is Colin, and I think he's from Europe and very old. Maybe several hundred years old even. And he is beautiful! About 5'8, thin and with almost delicate bones. His hair is mostly brown and curly. It was tied back like those guys in the Revolutionary war days. And his eyes! I can't begin to describe the brown depths, it's like looking into a huge cup of hot chocolate with just the right amount of milk.

At first, he was pissed that I was following him, but I was able to explain myself, and we made a deal. I have some research to do, and then I'm ready. I can't wait. I will be the skinny and beautiful woman I always wanted to be. We have a meeting tonight.

That was the end of the journal.

Willie was silent for a while. "This answers a lot, Reba. Why didn't you let me read it before?"

"I wasn't sure it was real. Would you have believed it? Remember, we didn't know then what we know now. Your dream decided it for me. Way too much like Gwen's for me not to make the connection." They sat in quiet contemplation of the genuine possibility that not only were vampires real, but their friend was a blood drinker while it got darker and more people started crowding the streets.

Willie and Reba watched the people wandering the street; most of them were tourists let off their leash, and some of them were quite drunk by the time the sun began to sink below the horizon. They played an old game of "Who is sober and who is good at pretending" they had invented years ago during their clubbing days. "Look at that guy over there." Reba pointed at a man clad in shorts and sandals with socks. "He has such gravitas. I say he is drunk."

Willie studied the man before answering. "Nope, he is sober." Reba looked askance at him.

"Really? He is setting each foot down with such elaborate care he has to be tipsy!"

"Nope, look behind him. The young girl running to catch up with him. She has his cane." Sure enough, the cane belonged to the careful gentleman and once he accepted it, his stride became much more confident. "Ya gotta look beyond the person itself. Sometimes there is an outside influence."

Reba mock punched his shoulder, and they both grinned. "Here comes someone, he's a nice looking chap, well dressed, slim and if I can say it, beautiful." Willie turned to see this beautiful man.

"That guy over there? In the black pants and shirt?" He sighed. "Yeah, he is beautiful."

"Put your tongue back in your mouth man!" laughed Reba. "We're here for another reason. He almost looks like he's from another time, his hair is long, and he walks as if the world should give way to him. Oh, he's stopped."

They both looked a little surprised at that, Willie more than Reba. "Will ya look at the way he stands. Excellent posture, hands clasped in front. He has a downright sereneness feel to him as if he has forever to wait for whatever it is, he's waiting for."

"Um, Willie." Reba tapped her finger on Willie's hand. "What?"

"Look closer. Does he look familiar to you? I mean, do you have the feeling we have seen him before?" Narrowing his eyes to focus better in the deepening gloom, Willie peered as closely as he could at the figure standing on the corner.

He gasped. "You're right! He does look familiar. Why? We don't know anyone in New Orleans."

"We know at least two people in New Orleans and that guy was with one of them."

"Don't get all mysterious on me, Reba. What do you mean?"

"I mean, that is the guy we've seen watching the boarding house." Willie still looked confused. "You know, the guy with the woman that looked so much like Gwen, the one that fits the description of Gwen's vampire perfectly."

Another long look. "Oh my god! You're right! He's the guy who stood on the corner. He gave me the creeps. What d'ya think he's doing here now?"

The answer came a minute later when a beautiful woman also in black appeared by the mysterious black-clad man. She was a thin copy of Gwen. From short height down to the funny pigeon-toed walk that got Gwen laughed at so much in her past. It was the slightly stumbling walk that convinced Reba. Breathless, she could only grip Willie's hands tight. "Willie, Willie....I think...oh my god...I don't know what to think! It can't be. But it has to be! There has got to be another reason!"

"Another reason for what, Reba. You're getting me scared here. Reason for what?"

"I think the woman over there is Gwen."

"Nah, she's too thin. We just saw her last night, and she was still fat. No way she lost all that weight in one night!" He laughed. "If she did, she's onto something really good."

Reba stared pointedly at them and spoke slowly. "Something really good? Like vampires being such gorgeous creatures?" His jaw dropped, and he turned his head to see the couple across the street. Who was looking straight at him and Reba.

Across the street, the aristocratic man in black leaned over and said something to the Gwen looking woman. She seemed to argue with him and shook her head now but his will prevailed and they stepped into the street to cross, the Gwen looking woman dragging a little bit behind.

Panic rooted Reba and Willie to the bench. On the one hand, this might [yeah right] be just a case of two people wondering why they were being stared at. On the other hand, these were vampires coming right at them! Panic is not a fun sensation. Willie had never experienced it before. He was pretty sure Reba hadn't either. They did now. Actually, neither of them were thinking. Not with the part of the brain that controls logical thought at least.

The more primitive part of the brain took over, they gasped for air, and their hearts tried to pound out of their chests. The logical mind was telling them 'this is not happening, those are not vampires, such creatures don't exist.' But the primitive brain was screaming 'vampires gonna suck your blood!' It took a few seconds before any body parts reacted and by then the couple was standing in front of them. The man spoke. "I think it is time we had a discussion.

Chapter Twenty-Seven

"May we sit down?" The man in black gestured at the rest of the bench. When the two did little more than open their mouths like fish gasping for air he spoke again. "We can remain standing, but it would make you uncomfortable, and would interfere with what we have to say." A shaky wave of Reba's hand and they sat down. The man looked at Gwen's double as if to say, 'your turn.'

Gwen's double gave a weak wave. "Hi, Reba. Hi Willie. Guess you want to know more, right?" At their woozy nods, she went on. "I'll start at the beginning. The best place to start, I guess. You know I came here to find vampires. I wasn't really sure, but I kept looking and if you know where and how you can find traces. Well, I did. And that turned out to be Colin here." She indicated the black-clad man who, thankfully did not grin in response, but acknowledged the introduction with an uplifted eyebrow.

"Long story short, I begged him to make me a vampire because I wanted to be beautiful and finally, he agreed to 'turn' me into a vampire. He needed help in the computer age, and I could give him that help."

Willie interrupted. "But you're still fat! We saw you last night!" He blushed when he realized what he had said and then paled when he realized what he had said it to.

"As to that, I'm afraid, for me, it isn't that easy. Apparently, if I feed"... a few shudders from her audience..."...if I feed too much then I revert to my original state. Which is overweight. I have to be careful how many times I feed"... again a shudder from her audience.... "How many times I feed so I don't revert."

Reba spoke both her and Willie's take. "Does that mean you have to diet? Forever?"

Gwen rolled her eyes a bit. "Yes. It means I have to diet forever."

The two sat quietly for a while, digesting Gwen's revelations. Reba glanced at Gwen. "But if..." she sighed and looked down at her sneakers.

Next, it was Willie's turn to try to express. "Why didn't you...?" His shoes suddenly got very interesting to him too. Then they both spoke stepping over each other.

"What about Em..."

"I don't understand..."

"This is all so unbelievable…"

Angrily Gwen hissed, "I never expected you to believe me! That's why I stopped calling. You all thought I was going crazy. Admit it. And as for Emily, who told her? Who got her involved? Huh? Tell me that! All I ever wanted was to be left alone. Now you got my sister involved and who knows what's gonna happen. A shit show is gonna happen, and the three of you are right in the middle of it!" Her voice broke, and she covered her face with her perfectly manicured hands.

"A shit show? What do you mean?" Both Willie and Reba jumped to the feet, Willie looking around him frantically as if a dozen vampires were sneaking up on them and he couldn't decide whether he wanted to punch someone or run.

Colin motioned them both to sit down. "Gwen has explained to you what she has done and what she has become. And now you know. There is a lot to explain that even Gwen doesn't know and little time to tell you what you need to know. Since you are now caught up in this, you need to know the story.

He leaned into the three listeners; his brown eyes shadowed beneath his brows. Only a faint gleam could be seen as he opened his lips and began speaking.

"First. Yes. Vampires are real. You are not hallucinating; your friend is one of us."

He sat back and watched Willie and Reba digest the information, which they did with remarkable alacrity. "Second. Gwen's sister has unfortunately gotten herself kidnapped by a coven and need your help."

Gwen's friends erupted. "Emily is in danger?"

"Is she gonna be 'turned'?"

Colin held his hand up. "Third. There is a large coven active in New Orleans with whom I have unfortunately had dealings with in the past, or at least dealings with the leader of the coven. I won't go into details. All you need to know right now is they are a particularly nasty bunch. I was suspicious of them possibly being here when the missing people reports started growing, but I had no way to know for sure."

"So how do you know now?" Willie asked.

Colin pointed across the street to the infamous bar. "Do you see that drab, grey-clad individual over there? The one standing very still as if waiting for orders to move?" Reba and Willie nodded, they had seen several of those persons earlier and thought it strange to see someone so inanimate in New Orleans.

"Yeah? What about them?" Colin's look of disdain silenced Willie.

Eternal Diet — Wendy Wilson

"I have seen many of those drabs before in my time. You are knowledgeable enough about us to know the movies have it wrong about how vampires are made, I hope. It is not simply a matter of the amount of times blood is drunk from a victim; we choose to turn or not turn by giving our protégé our blood after we have drunk from them. If we take only small amounts of blood, we gain mental and psychic control of a person; the more times, the more powerful the control. We take a little blood, and we do not give them ours. That is how vampire slaves are made."

This was almost too much for the two friends. Varying levels of vampirism! A dozen questions ripped through their minds, and again, they both burst out in unison, their questions tumbling one over the other.

"Why do vampires…"

"How do you know…."

"What are they used….."

And the most important. "Why are you telling us this now?"

"We are telling you this now because despite my best efforts…" Colin looked accusingly at Gwen. "…despite my best efforts to prevent it, you are now involved. And more, unfortunately, Gwen's sister is involved. There is indeed a 'shit storm,' as it has been so inelegantly put, approaching.

In the past, I have had dealings with the type of vampire that creates those drabs, and I fear another group has begun again and they aim to enslave humans, one city at a time, apparently starting with New Orleans.

"Why New Orleans? Wouldn't a bigger city be easier to hide in?"

Colin looked at Willie approvingly and nodded. "Yes, I am surprised to see them here as well, I would have thought a larger city would have more anonymity, but I realize there is one thing here that other cities do not have." He chuckled softly at the three focused faces. Even Gwen leaned in to hear. "Actually, it is several things. Other cities have one or more of these attributes, but they come together so very well here. First; New Orleans is a tourist city famous for its drinking and dining excesses. Many people are attracted to the atmosphere, so there is a large transient population that is difficult for authorities to track.

"Another reason is the climate; usually warm enough for people to be out in the streets, which in large portions of the city, are poorly lit and even less protected by the police. That makes it easy to stalk and overtake a victim who has, shall we say, overindulged at a bar? A large homeless population as a result of the mild weather, having little need for stout houses and comfortably living on the streets almost invites us to take advantage of them.

"The river and lake are close by so many of the victims of blood drinkers are written off as victims of drowning when disposed of in that way. There are other reasons including mythology and recent storytelling that attract my brethren as well to New Orleans, but that will suffice for now. Any one of those reasons would draw a vampire, but when put all together it makes the city almost irresistible."

"So what you're saying is it's a confluence of differing attractions making it something like a perfect storm, right?"

Again Colin looked approvingly at Willie. "You understand. Yes. The general casual attitude of the Southern regions and the freedom of morality here in this city is unique. There is also a large population who follows religions that not only do not deny us, but actively believe in us. Trust me, it makes a person feel most welcome when his kind is actively admired, and vampires are no exception to vanity."

There it was. The definitive explanation by the one individual who would know the why and how of what was happening. Reba and Willie could not deny the evidence before their own eyes of Gwen transforming overnight. She had come to New Orleans to find vampires and had found them. It wasn't Gwen playing a joke on them and pretending she had been turned into a vampire because they had seen with their own eyes the incredible change from overweight and frumpy to lean and svelte. It just doesn't happen that fast. No way, no how. The legends were true. And their friend was proof. Now what?

They accepted the truth of the matter, no matter how incredible it sounded. But that left a central question; what were they going to do to save Emily. She was apparently mixed up with this and judging by the timeline suggested by Colin in how easy it was to gain control over a person, they did not have a great deal of time to act.

Reba ventured with the first question. "I believe Emily is somehow involved with this coven you mentioned. In fact, I am sure of it. This is the bar she investigated, and now she is missing. She's in a lot of danger, isn't she?" It was hard to keep the tremor of fear out of her voice, but she took a deep breath, let it out slowly and continued. "What can we do? Is she a vampire now too? Do you even know where she is?"

Gwen answered. "She hasn't been turned. Yet." The two mortals jumped on it. Where was she, how did she know Emily was safe, what was she going to do to save her sister and if she hadn't been turned then what did they want with her?

"She is being held as bait." Colin's voice cut through the mish-mash of voices and silenced them. "And Gwen knows where."

"Yes! I know where she is. What I don't know is how to get her out. I almost got caught myself and only just got away. She's not hurt, but she is scared, I'll tell you that."

With Willie and Reba anxiously trying hard not to grab her by the neck and shake the information out of her, Gwen told them all she knew. She explained how she had followed the woman bartender and minion to a large, abandoned mansion a few miles out of town in the swamps. How far back it was set from the lonely country road, it was on and how the woodwork was falling off because of damp rot and brick were covered with mold.

The picture of a noble old plantation fallen on hard times grew in the listener's minds. The old cypress trees dripping with Spanish moss growing up out of the swampy mud. They could almost hear insects of all kind buzzing around and the hoot of owls hunting for dinner. Gwen apparently had a talent for story telling they had been unaware of.

She described her climb up the bricks onto an upper window ledge and hearing Emily crying behind one of the black painted windows. Her mortal listeners grasped their own fingers when she told of the screeching when she tried to scrape the paint with her fingernails and her happiness when she had, at last, cleared a space big enough to gaze through. It was at this point she choked up a bit.

"That's ok," Reba said as she stroked Gwen's forearm. "Go on and tell the rest."

"I had just cleared a little peephole and looked in. Emily had stopped crying but the room was dark, and I couldn't see her at first. Then her eye was in the peephole, and she saw me. We didn't have time for anything but for her to recognize me and yell my name. Someone burst into her room and yanked her away, and all I could do was drop down and run.

I don't understand how I got away, but I did. There were so many of them, it was like a swarm!" She turned to Colin. "They let me go, I think. You're right. Emily is being held as bait. But why? And what do you and me have to do with it? What does she want from us? She's never even heard of me!"

The three turned to Colin who seemed to be uncomfortable under their combined gaze. "I have told you I am familiar with this coven. What I haven't told you is that I was once a part of it." Complete amazed silence. Except for Gwen.

She sighed. "Ah, so that's why you avoid every vampire in the city!"

"You should know by now that WE vampires." He looked very sternly at Gwen. "WE vampires are solitary. Except for the fledgling's training and the fulfillment of whatever contract involved in the turning, vampires do not associate with others of our kind. Do not base your knowledge of us by our interaction. We will part company eventually." Gwen looked almost devastated. She hadn't discovered this fact in her research.

"But what about the coven?" Willie asked. "If vampires don't do groups why did these form a coven?"

"Sometimes a vampire of ancient lineage and great power will force the younger and weaker of our kind to follow his or her will. You must understand that the older we are, the more powerful we become. As time goes on, we gain in abilities and skills. It takes millennia, but the Madame I speak of is one of the most ancient vampires on earth. I know of none older or more powerful. And I think I know why she has kidnapped your sister, Gwen."

"Why?"

"Because she wants me."

That stopped them. Why would an ancient and powerful vampire go to the trouble to lure another run of the mill vampire that just happened to be in the city? They could understand why recruiting vampires helped her but why make such a special effort? Kidnapping was a messy crime and often ended badly for all involved. Even Gwen didn't know what made Colin so special that the Madame was willing to involve the authorities just to reach him. They could not figure it out.

Colin watched the thoughts flicker across the three friends faces. And decided to tell them. They all had a right to know. "In my native country, I was a nobleman. Merely a third son perhaps but born to a noble family and as such had wealth and influence. My father had me educated in arms and weaponry, and my planned fate was to serve in the military.

However, no one asked me what I wanted so I rejected the family and sought my own future. I ended up in financial and social trouble. A savior appeared, or at least that's what she looked to be. My breeding and family connections were valuable to her, and she befriended me. As a young and foolish man with little experience in the world outside of the upper classes, I was ripe for picking. And pick me she did.

"I will not go into detail; we have little time for my confession, but when Madame seduced and turned me, I wholeheartedly entered into her world. Servants were common in my home, so it was a while before I grasped exactly what I came to call her 'minions' were. They were little more than brainless bodies doing her will and a convenient source of ready blood. Even then, it was a long time before I became disgusted with the practice and when I learned of Madame's ultimate goal, I had to reconsider my connection with her."

He stopped talking and gave them a minute to take in what he had told them. It was the first time he had ever shared his history with anyone in his long existence as a blood drinker. For not the first time Colin wondered what it was about Gwen that made him seek her approval and, dare he think it, her love. He had met so many women and men in his long life; it was impossible to remember them all. Being around Gwen had undoubtedly stirred up memories he had long suppressed. No time to dwell on the fleeting images and thoughts that spun through his subconscious.

Eternal Diet   *Wendy Wilson*

"My conscience, which I thought had been long buried arose. I could no longer stand by, let alone actively participate, in the enslavement of my own countrymen and women. I broke with Madame and by doing so she lost the influence my position afforded her. It did not please her, and I had to flee my homeland.

For many years I wandered Europe until I heard rumors of a spectacularly powerful vampire living in the swamps of the New World and I decided to search for this blood brother." He chuckled. "The end result is I came to New Orleans and that, my friends, is enough about my history. It is clear though that Madame has discovered my whereabouts and has decided to find me. She is vengeance incarnate, and I shudder to think her eye is on me and my protégé."

During this long monologue, the crowds in the street had started to thin, it was getting late, and dawn was only a few hours away. Nothing of interest had happened at the bar; no minion, no vampire, no indication of anything out of the ordinary at all. It was just like every other bar in the city; fun with good drinks and an occasional drunk being kicked out.

Gwen looked at the quiet streets and decided it was time to act. "I think it's time Reba and Willie get a more first-hand look at the place my sister is."

"Why do you want us to do that?" Both of the mortals were a bit surprised at Gwen's declaration of what they needed to do. After all, not a few hours ago they were ready to leave for home. "What can we do?"

Colin explained. "No plans have been made, but we think you should at least be shown the property. Gwen knows where the house is and since she has no ties to anyone there but her sister, no vampire will be able to sense her any more than they can any other vampire. If I were to bring you there, Madame would know before we were a mile away."

Gwen pleaded with her now beautiful, dark-rimmed eyes. "Will you at least come with me to see the place?" Willie and Reba had no choice but to agree for no one can withstand a vampire's will, especially if she is your best friend.

An hour later the trio paused at the junction of a dirt country road through the swamp and an overgrown path with a chain across it. Their flashlights illuminated the sign, which read "No Trespassing." Beyond the chain and sign, the path narrowed to a mere path with cypress trees dripping with Spanish moss over hanging from the wetlands on either side. All sorts of grass and flora grew between the trees. It was clear that no car or cart had traveled this road regularly. "This is the path to the house. We can't go any closer than this though." Gwen indicated the winding path.

"It's only a few hundred yards down that way."

"Why are you showing us this?" Willie asked. "What can we do?"

"Don't you want to know where Emily is? Maybe you can get the cops to come out here. Maybe you can rescue her."

They stood there in the quiet for a minute. The only sounds were those of the frogs and insects. An occasional distant grunt and splash of an alligator sliding into the water reminding them that other things were abroad. Reba flapped her arms at the swarms of mosquitoes around her. "Ah! Get away, you awful bloodsucking fiends!" She realized what she had said and, with a grimace of guilt looked at Gwen.

Who laughed. "That's ok, they are fiends! Let's get you back into town before you turn into one huge mosquito bite." The two gratefully followed her back down the dirt road until they were within the city limits. "It's time for me to go, I have to 'sleep' now."

"Where should we meet tonight?" Reba asked.

"Let's make it the fountain in the park, if we are seen at the bar again, it might arouse suspicion.

"Ok. The fountain it is." They parted company and left to finish what they could of the night.

Chapter Twenty-Eight

The boarding house door was locked, and dead bolted tightly as Reba and Willie went in and slowly climbed the stairs to the room. Dawn was barely an hour away, and they were both dead tired. Reba yawned and stretched. "I think I could sleep until noon."

"Whatta ya mean, sleep?" Willie sounded astonished. "We can't sleep now; we have to go back!"

"Back where?"

"To the mansion. Why else did Gwen and her, hell, I don't know WHAT to call him, make such a point of showing us where the house was? They want us to go back and kill Madame! We are the only ones who can. Vampires 'sleep' during the day, mortals are awake."

Understanding dawned on Reba's face. "You're right! I was just so damn tired I didn't even think of that. Vampires are helpless in the daytime, and now that we know where their lair is, we can kill the leader." She stopped and looked at Willie, who was walking around the room searching for something. "Whatcha looking for?"

Willie stopped lifting boxes and opening cupboards. "What's the one sure fire way to kill a vampire?" "Everyone knows that… put a stake through the heart. Psssh. It's doesn't take a genius to know that."

Reba sighed. "Willie, do you see anything remotely resembling a stake in this room? How about a hammer?" His face fell and she felt sorry for him. "No. Look, Willie, we are both so exhausted neither of us is thinking straight. You're actually looking for vampire killing equipment in a boarding house. Let's sleep a few hours and then go to a hardware store and get what we need and then go kill us a vampire." They set the alarm for 10 am, and both of them dropped into their beds and within a few minutes were sound asleep.

The woman was close; Willie knew it in his soul. The profound odor of something dead and decaying drifted around him, sending foul tendrils into his nose. He sneezed. Softly the intricate melody of a Chopin opus began to play on a piano. The player was skilled, and judging by the quality of sound, it must have come from a full-size concert piano.

Eternal Diet — *Wendy Wilson*

Arms outstretched trying to feel, in the complete and utter darkness, something that would help him. Anything that would tell him where he was, and how to get out would be of help. A glimmer of light flared in the distance. He knew at once what it was and turned away. The light came closer. His limbs were heavy, slow to move as if in a block of almost frozen ice.

He sensed her presence. She was close, willing him to turn and face her. His will broke against her granite strength and he as it did; he turned to see what had tormented his dreams. Enough, his mind screamed for relief. Give in and be with her. It was more than he could bear. Closer she came, smoothly as if on a cloud, a black thundercloud ready to erupt and engulf him as he stood rooted waiting for her embrace.

She spoke. Her voice was the call of ancient beings enticing humanity to reject the Garden of Eden and stand with knowledge and power. "Come to me. I can offer you life everlasting." His will shattered, he reached for her. She reached for him.

"Hey, lazybones! C'mon. Get up. The alarm's been ringing at least a minute. Didn't you hear it?" Reba shook Willie's shoulder. "I was in the bathroom when it went off. What, didn't you hear it? Were you

Eternal Diet   *Wendy Wilson*

that out of it?" Willie swung his feet over the edge of his cot and onto the floor. He sat there feeling the solidness of the wood, sweeping his big toe along the joint between two planks. Listening to the whirrrr of the fan. Being in the room and being alive. Reba studied him. "What's wrong? You look like you've seen a ghost. Did you have another dream?"

"No, I..I... I didn't. I guess I was just, so very tired." Now, why did he deny it? He didn't want to explore his denial, so he got up and went into the bathroom. Reba had left the shower steaming up the little room, and he stripped and turned the water back on. Oh! Blessed water cascading onto his skin, cleansing it of the dream. At the end he turned off the hot water and stood under the cold stream, pretending it was a mountain waterfall. By the time he was toweled off and back into the room the dream was just a puff of smoke drifting in his mind. More important things to think about. "So, breakfast and then Ace Hardware?"

"Sounds good to me."

By noontime they were dressed, fed, shopped out, and ready to go. Sledgehammer and wooden dowel in hand they began their walk. "Wait a minute." Called Willie to Reba who was a few feet ahead.

Eternal Diet   *Wendy Wilson*

"What's wrong? Did we forget something?" In answer, Willie lifted the 1-inch dowel so she could clearly see the end and, with a lift of his eyebrows, waved it lightly. "Stop waving that thing around, Willie. You're gonna bonk me over the head with it!"

"Right! Bonk someone over the head is about all this stick can do."

Understanding dawned on her. "Oh! Yes. That thing is flat at the end, we need it pointy, like a sword or a sharp pencil. Preferably stronger than a sharp pencil. Do you have a pocket knife? We could trim it."

"What, do I look like McGyver? Of course I don't have a pocketknife! We have to go back to the store and get one. Damn!"

So the two of them turned and trudged back down the way they had just come and went back to the hardware store. Which, they found, was closed for lunch. A sign on the door said "Closed for Lunch. See You Then" The arms of the cute little clock in the middle had been moved to 1:30. "A fine lot of vampire hunters was are! Van Helsing would be spinning."

"Do you want to wait or look for another store?"

"Wait; it was hard enough to find this one. At least we can sit in the cafe across the street and be cool."

Eternal Diet *Wendy Wilson*

At least the cafe was air-conditioned, and the flavored coffees and brioche they got were a delicious way to top off their earlier quickie breakfast. Reba kept twisting her wrist to look at her watch. "A watched pot never boils." Willie intoned with great seriousness. And they both broke out in giggles.

"A watched pot may never boil but a watched store inevitably re-opens." Reba elbowed Willie and nodded to the store, and they both slid out of the booth and crossed the street to the store.

"Ya looking for a pocket knife, are ya? Got a bunch of 'em rightcheer." The elderly store clerk, who was wearing a badge that said 'Hi My Name Is Guillaume' bent down and opened a locked case and lifted up a display of knives of varying sizes onto the counter. "Gotta be careful with sharp things nowadays. Kids will steal just about anything not locked up, and they love the knives. Oh, yes indeed. They love the knives. Dangerous and small, perfect for all sorts of trouble making."

He peered through thick glasses at the two in front of him. Who were shuffling their feet in their desire to just get a knife and get on with the vampire slaying. "What did you say you wanted it for? Wasn't you in here before getting a rubber hammer and a dowel?"

"Yeah, that was us." Answered Willie; as the male involved in the transaction, he had the most authority within this setting. Even though he had never wielded a knife for more than cutting his meat and vegetables. "I'm gonna do some, some..." He peeked at Reba looking for help. She made little swiping motions as if she was peeling a cucumber or squash. "...Some whittling! Yeah. I wanna just sit on the porch and whittle away."

The old man scrunched up his face, clearly not believing the claim but, a sale was a sale, so he got on with it. "This here knife is just right for fine work..."

"No, I need a bigger blade; the wood I'm gonna whittle is pretty dense. And larger. Quite large in fact."

"Lookie here, you ain't planning on whittling that dowel I sold ya, are ya? That ain't the kina wood you use for that!"

"Does it matter? I just need a knife, please." Willie pointed at a large hunting knife. "That one should do well." Guillaume shrugged and handed Willie the knife.

"$29.99. With tax..." He punched the register. "$32.86. Cash or credit?"

The two sat on a bench down the street from the shop, and Willie broke out the knife and dowel and began to slice away the wood at the end trying to form a point. It was hard going, and soon he noticed that passerbys were looking strangely at him. "Hey, Reba. I think we need to get further out of the city. I feel like these people half expect me to jump up and chase them with the knife and sharp, pointy stick."

Reba studied the way tourists sped up when they realized what Willie was doing. One couple even tandem lifted and dragged their toddler as quickly as they could pass. The child screamed with delight. "Again!" Her Dad picked her up and distracted her with a cookie as he and Mom put on the steam to full power walk.

By the time the friends had sharpened the dowel and found their way to the old mansion it was later than they had planned. "It's late afternoon, Willie. And we don't know exactly where Madame's coffin is. We can't go stumbling around. Why don't we just try to get Emily and get out?"

"I know where the coffin is," Willie answered in a flat, low, voice. "You go look for Emily, Gwen said she's on the third floor. I'm gonna find Madame."

"What do ya mean you know where Madame is? How?"

"Never mind how, I just do. You find Emily and get her away. I'll take care of Madame." He hugged her and, carrying stake and sledge, led the way around the building looking for the best way in.

They hopped the brick wall that seemed remarkably well kept and crossed to the house and came to a stone stairway leading down into what appeared to be a basement. A basement? In the swamps of New Orleans? They looked closer and realized they had been slowly climbing a constructed uprise in the grounds and what looked like a stairway underground was, in reality, a stairway down a few steps. It would probably be the level of "Downstairs" viewers familiar with "Downton Abbey" and similar shows would recognize.

At the bottom was a locked door. "Of course it's locked. Couldn't make this easy for us." Willie snorted at Reba's attempt at humor and brandished his brand new hunting knife.

"This will work I bet. I did WATCH enough McGyver shows to know how to do shit." Placing the blade carefully within one of the rungs of the chain he twisted it until they heard a 'snap.' "That's got it." Reba shushed him.

"Wait a minute. That made noise. Hide and see if anything comes to look." They tiptoed up the stairs and hid behind the corner of the building. Nothing. It was safe.

Eternal Diet   *Wendy Wilson*

It was only a matter of minutes until Willie had pulled the chain and the door swung open. They both carefully slid their feet along the concrete floor and looked around at the room they were in. It was a lot like the rooms seen in the TV shows of wealthy aristocrats in England where the help didn't mingle with the helped except when absolutely necessary.

Number one, the windows were all blacked out, it was impossible to see anything beyond five feet, and that was because the door was still open. Once that was closed, they would be in complete darkness.

"Glad we each have a flashlight!" Reba whispered as she clicked hers on. Willie closed the door and then clicked his light on. They both turned in a 360-degree circle looking at the room they were in. Cages were lined up along one side of the room. They were barely large enough to house a large dog. The sides went up to the ceiling, and they wondered if it was to prevent dogs from climbing out.

"Look over here Willie!" Reba was shining her light into one of the cages. "I don't think these were used for keeping dogs." The cage he was looking in had a raised cot and some blankets. On the wall were scratchings looking a bit like hashtags at first glimpse.

Reba squinted her eyes and gasped. Willie focused on the wall and gasped too. "Those marks were made by a person! Someone was kept down here!" Reba whispered as loud as she dared to him from another cage. "Look! There's more marks in this one. And this one." Their flashlights scoured each cage along the walls. At the last one, the blanket moved.

Willie dropped his flashlight and dove for it. Reba's light stayed steady. Willie came up with a flashlight in one hand and stake and hammer in the other. Mumbling something about 'damn fingers not working…' he bent down and placed the stake and hammer on the floor and joined Reba in shining a light into the tiny cell.

The blanket moved, and a pale and weak arm emerged. The arm pushed back the cover to reveal a person, well, almost a person, trying to sit up. It was not an animal but not quite a human either. Reba recognized it first. "I know what that is! It's one of those minions Colin was telling us about!" The minion peered at them through the bars of the cell, lifting his arm to ward off the stark brilliance of the dual lights. "Oh, sorry." They lowered the beams and stared.

The creature stared back. There was something about this minion that was a little bit different from the others; there was a spark of intelligence in its eyes. "Wh, who, who are you?" it stuttered as it cowered as

Eternal Diet   *Wendy Wilson*

far from the bars as it could. "Go away. Leave me alone. Please dun't hurt me anymore."

"Who's hurting you?" This startled it. Apparently, no one had asked it a question in a long time. There were bruises all up and down where ever the shapeless garment of oversized blouse and pants didn't cover. But the most obvious wounds were the bite marks on its wrists and neck. Some of which looked quite recent.

"They are hurting me. Aren't you one of them?"

"Oh, honey we aren't here to hurt you." Reba turned to Willie. "Get the knife and break the lock."

Releasing Luc, for that was the creature's name, was done in a minute. He crept outside, ready to run if either of them made any move. Standing in the slightly better light, it was clear he was only in his mid-teens since his height was little more than a few inches above five feet, but he didn't have the characteristic soft features of a child.

His nose was broad as was his shoulders and his muscles came from physical labor, not playing soccer in the local league like a more pampered teen might show. Black-brown eyes and a loose curl to his dark hair marked him as a Creole and probably a native of the city.

Along with the bruises, the two friends noticed several puncture marks on Luc's arms and his neck. Noticing where they were looking, he quickly folded his arms over his chest and dropped his chin down. "Dun't hurt me. Please. Dun't bite me."

Willie and Reba exchanged amazed looks. Reba tried to give him a hug, but Luc slithered as far away as he could without ending up back in the cage. "Jus let me go. I wun't tell nobody 'bout dis place!"

"But that's just it, Luc; we want to know about this place. We won't hurt you."

Reba spoke in a soothing voice, and when Luc relaxed, even going as far as to stand like he was ready to hit something, she went on. "You might be able to help us. A friend of ours is being kept here."

"Then she's one of them. Or one of the others; what they trying to turn me into. Y'all too late." He shrugged off Reba's hug. "Do y'all wanna help your friend? Then kill the mutha fuckas."

"What have they been doing to you?" Willie gestured to Luc's wounds. "I mean it looks like they've been drinking your blood. Why aren't you one of the mindless slaves that work here?"

Luc shrugged again. "Dunno. I just know they been tryin' but it's not been workin'. Heard 'em say I'm too smart or 'wrong-headed.'" He gave a small laugh. "Be the firs time anybody called me smart! Been called 'wrong-headed enough so mebbe thas it. I don' listen to what people tell me ta do. 'Wrong-headed'! Thas funny."

Reba tried again. "I don't think Emily has been injured. We have reason to believe she's here as bait. She would have come here sometime last week. Her sister saw her in a third story window so as of two nights ago she was ok."

"Oh! I think I know what you talkin bout! Jus the other night there was a great big ruckus here. Heard some talk 'bout somebody sneaking around. You shoulda seen those fuckas flying around!"

They had all been speaking in a whisper, and when Luc's laugh threatened to break out of quiet mode, Willie put his hand on his mouth. Luc nodded, and Willie dropped his hand. "I know you want to get away but can you help us find our friend?"

Big-eyed and closed lipped, Luc nodded and pointed upstairs. "I been upstairs a coupla times. Enough to know how to get to the stairs. Follow me."

Together they all crept up the stairs, and Luc slowly pushed the door open. It was dark in the room but not the stygian black of the downstairs. Flashlights flipped off, the three let their eyes adjust to the level of light. Willie tapped Reba, and with elaborate hand signals he told her to go with Luc to find Emily and motioned that he would search the floor they were on. She frantically gestured for him to come with her and Luc, but he shook his head no, pointed to himself and indicated he was going to look around. Finally, Reba reluctantly nodded, and they separated, wondering if they would ever see each other again.

Halfway down the corridor Luc grabbed Reba's arm and pulled her into a dark corner. His eyes told her "Shh." Not a moment later she heard a small scuffling footfall of someone coming down a flight of stairs. Reba crouched down and make herself as small as she could, but it was clear the corner wasn't going to hide both of them. Luc then did something strange. He stood a step away from the corner and stood, arms hanging loose and his posture slightly stooped, staring into space with blank eyes and open mouth in front of and blocking Reba from view.

The minion, for minion it was, came down the stairs and passed Luc without a bit of reaction. It was if he wasn't there. As soon as it had passed, Luc straightened up and grabbed Reba's hand. "C'mon, we gotta move. They stupid but will attack anything not belonging here."

"Why didn't that one ask you what you were doing just standing there?"

"A lotta them jus stand around waitin for orders. Normal for em. Les go, the coast is clear."

Apparently, the vampires inhabiting the house believed their slaves and the compunction laid on them to attack anything other than those who dwelt in the house was sufficient protection against daytime invasion because they didn't run into anything other than two more minions and both times Luc managed to fool them by his act.

They just went about their business, cleaning and carrying things about the house, oblivious to their surroundings. At the top of the third floor, Luc made sure the hall was empty and turned to Reba. "I'm gonna go. Thank you for gettin me outta that cage. I paid you back by bringin you here. We even. I ain't goin any futher. Bonne chance." With that, he crept down the stairs and out of sight.

Reba waited for Luc's footsteps to go padding down the stairs until she couldn't hear them anymore. Then she turned her attention to the reason she was there; finding Emily. There were three rooms on either side of the hall. Which one to pick, which one...

She couldn't just go around opening doors at random because who knew what was behind any one door? She certainly didn't. Gwen had said she could hear Emily crying so maybe listening at each door would give her a clue. With no better plan of action, she decided to go with the listening.

The first door she listened at was silent. Nothing at all. Same for the next two. As she walked towards the last two rooms, she heard a shuffling. Was it coming from one of the two remaining rooms or was it a minion on patrol? The sound was so faint it could have been coming from anywhere. No time to decide, she had to move fast. Reaching for the doorknob, she realized this one had a lock on it. This had to be Emily's room. The key was in the lock! As quietly and quickly as she could, she turned the key and knob and entered the room.

She paused at the doorway. If she walked in on something other than Emily who knew what might happen. She didn't want to find that out.

A faint "Reba? Is that really you?" told her she had lucked out; this was where they were keeping Emily. The two women hugged and hugged and then broke away to look at each other. And then they hugged some more. "You came!"

Reba immediately shushed her. "We can't make noise, the minions are all over the place, and Luc says they will attack anyone who doesn't belong here."

Emily nodded and opened the door a crack just large enough to see if anyone or thing was in the hall.

"Coast is clear. But I don't know the way, they always blindfolded me."

"That's ok, I know how to get out. We just gotta be careful and not make noise."

Everything went well until they came to the bottom of the staircase. There they heard what could only be yet another minion coming towards them. They were trapped in the open; their choice was to run back up the stairs and hope nothing heard them or brazen it out and try to outrun the minion. It didn't take long to decide. No way were they going back upstairs to be caught in a dead end. Just to be sure though, they edged as close as they could to the corner; no need to attract attention. Emily stood just a bit in front of Reba.

The shuffling got closer until the women could tell it was only a few feet away around the corner and would be able to see them in a few seconds. They clasped their hands together and waited. The creature stepped around the corner and saw the women. It raised its arm and opened its mouth as if to scream and indeed, a small screech did issue forth from the open lips. Before Reba and Emily could bolt past it, the minion closed its mouth, lowered its arm and stood meekly enough in front of them.

Eternal Diet *Wendy Wilson*

"What's he doing?" an amazed Emily asked. "What stopped him? Why isn't he attacking?"

An idea dawned in Reba's mind. "I think he's waiting for orders!"

"Whatta you mean 'orders'? I'm not his boss!"

"But you belong here! Don't you see?" Reba was delirious with relief. "It doesn't know you're not one of the bosses. You're certainly not one of them, and you live in the house, so that makes you, in their limited reality, a boss! Tell it to go upstairs. Go ahead, tell it." She pushed Emily to encourage her.

"Ok, ahhh." She put on her best 'boss' voice and spoke. "Go upstairs." And the minion turned away and climbed the stairs. It stopped at the top because she had not given any further orders, but it had obeyed Emily!

This was wonderful! They could safely get out of the building by merely ordering the minions to leave them alone! With Emily leading the way, they continued down one hall and up another until they came to the door to the 'cellar.' Only once more did they run into anything but with almost gleeful domination, Emily ordered it to join its fellow on the top of the stairs. "Ha! I almost wish there were more to order around!"

Reba was just happy to get as far as they had. "Be satisfied with what we got and let's vamoose!"

Soon after they had passed into the cellar, they heard the sound of an awfully loud bump and the discordant reverberations of a large piano being walloped on the floor above. "What the hell was that?" Both echoed the other. "We gotta move. Let's go." Without a backward glance, they both ran out of the house, over the fence and down the path as fast as they could run.

Emily pulled up when they reached the outskirts of town. She bent over, hands on knees and with deep breaths puffed out a stream of "Oh my god. I thought... I would never... get out of there! Do you know what they are...where's Gwen...thank you...oh my god...I have a million questions...what did they want with me... where is Gwen...what's going on... thank you... I'm going crazy... did you see…"

Reba guided Emily to a bench. "You're welcome. Now we wait for Willie. It's about two hours till sunset, he'll be along soon."

Emily lifted her head and, with eyes popping, shook her head. "Willie is in there? He isn't safe, Reba! Do you know what's in that place?"

"I have a pretty good idea. But everything is ok until sunset."

"No, it isn't. The leader of the group, the oldest woman I have ever seen, do you know anything about her?" Reba shook her head no. "During the day I could hear her moving around. She sometimes yelled at the slaves."

"But she's a vampire!" Reba objected.

"She may be a vampire but she's so old she doesn't need as much sleep and is awake a lot of the day. If Willie's in there, then he's in mortal danger."

Chapter Twenty-Nine

The sun set on New Orleans again, taking the sky full of white clouds and washing them with sky blue pinks. To the east a darker blue sky darkened from dark blue to purple to black; no moon tonight. The local night shift cops all finished their coffee and powered up their squad cars. The past few weeks had seen an increasing amount of missing people and mysteriously bloodless bodies dumped around town. They knew the ante was about to go up on a new moon night.

In a beautiful part of New Orleans where neighbors didn't bother the private lives of their neighbors, one of the denizens of the dark was just pushing back her covers. In her case, the cover was the top of her makeshift coffin. Her dainty feet swung over the side of the hope chest and slid onto the concrete floor of a room designed to be a bunker in times of distress. And she was distressed. The happenings of the past few days, well, for her, nights, had not stopped her from sleeping the sleep of the

Eternal Diet — Wendy Wilson

dead but now she was awake they swooped and dove at her like a hunting bat.

She knew her 'maker' was awake. His lid was up, and no one lay in it, so he was probably pacing waiting for her thoughts to be awake enough to make sense. This part confused her a little. He could read her mind, but she could not read his. He had explained it to her once. How vampires can 'hear' each other if they are close enough but cannot hear the thoughts of the one who 'made' them.

Most vampires, with some concentration, could hear human thought and a few, mostly the older ones, could impose their will upon humans. But why could she not hear him? Colin could not fully explain it, but it had something to do with his blood coursing through her veins gave him a connection stronger than any other, but it did not work in reverse. Not a good answer but all he could give her, and it had to do.

As usual, when she got to the top of the stairs, Colin was waiting for her in his sitting room. "I have a strange feeling, Gwen."

"What about?"

"About what your friends might have done today. I think they might have gotten themselves into trouble by entering the mansion."

"But didn't you want them to go there? I mean, isn't that what you were inferring the whole time you talked to them?" Colin sighed and motioned for Gwen to get ready to leave. She decided tonight was a night for sensible shoes and went into her 'bedroom' to change.

"I'm hungry." She announced when she came back out into the sitting room.

"You are always hungry." was his reply. "You of all people should know when to exercise restraint. I feel it is urgent for us to discover what happened during the day. You can feed later." With that, he went out the door and started walking quickly to the park where they had rendezvoused with Gwen's friends. Gwen sighed; picked up the keys Colin had uncharacteristically forgotten in his haste and locked the door behind her.

Colin and Gwen approached the park bench where they'd had their meeting several days earlier from behind. The two people sitting on the bench were silhouetted against the lights of the fountain. "Only two." Colin declared. "That means they didn't go then. I don't know whether to be relieved or disappointed."

From the slump of his shoulders, Gwen guessed it was the disappointment. "I'm disappointed too, that means my sister is...." The two people sitting on the bench turned at the sound of her voice. One was Reba, the other was... "EMILY!!!" Gwen's powerful vampiric voice drowned out the sound of the musicians, and everyone spun around to see the two women race to each other and enfold into an emotional hug. "Emily! You're safe!"

"Gwen! You're safe!"

The next few minutes were spent in tears with questions and answers spilling on top of each other. Questions were interrupted with sobs of joy and laughter. They spun around until Emily felt like a top. She had to stop, or she'd fall down. With Gwen finally releasing and allowing her to put her at arm's length, Emily got a good look at her sister. "My god, Gwen! When did you lose all that weight? You look incredible!"

"Gwen answered with a pat of her hair and a pert, "Don't I though?"

When things had calmed down to the point where they were no longer the focus of the crowd's attention, Reba motioned for the two newly reunited sisters to join them in a walk in the outskirts of the park. "C'mon girls. We got a lot to talk about." Reba let Gwen and Emily walk a little in front and couldn't help herself from scanning the crowd hoping to see a late coming familiar face. It didn't show. She knew what that probably meant and didn't want to be the one to tell the sisters.

The group walked until they found a private spot and Colin invited them to sit on a small bench the city had obviously forgotten about since it was rusty on the metal parts and needed sanding on the wooden parts. Nevertheless, they sat and looked expectantly at him.

He looked at Emily. "How much of what has happened in the past few weeks do you know about?"

She looked at Gwen and swallowed hard. "I know about what you are now. And I know what he is." She waved her hand at Colin. "You're vampires. You're not supposed to exist. But you do. I don't know what to believe anymore. My sister is a vampire."

"What we are is not the most important thing right now. What we are going to do is" The three women looked at Colin, a little amazed. Of course what he and Gwen were was central to this! "No. The most important thing right now is stopping the Madame and her coven." He looked at Reba to tell him even though he already knew the answer.

"Wasn't there a young man with you? Where is he now?"

"I don't know. We both went into the mansion but he, he didn't come out."

A small moan escaped Gwen. "He didn't come out? Then that means…."

"It means that the Madame has gotten to him and he is either dead or is now a vampire."

"There is one other option." Gwen sounded more hopeful than certain, but there was one chance… "He could be one of those slaves. And if he is, there's a chance we can save him, right? C'mon, don't look at me like that. Willie isn't a pushover, if they wanna use him as a slave, then it will take some time."

Reba perked up. "Yeah! A lot like that kid Luc!" She blinked at the quick looks from her audience. "Yeah, Luc was one of the guys they were trying to turn into a slave. It wasn't working so well with him, and he was able to help Willie and me."

"Do you know where this Luc is?" Colin asked as he paced up and down with his hand to his chin. "Would he be willing to help us?"

Reba shook her head. "He took off. Said he had paid for our help in getting him out when he got me to Emily's door. But he was in rough shape, he'd been beaten, and you could see the bite marks on his arm." Colin paced a little more, stopped and whirled around and pointed at Reba. She got a little nervous at the intensity in his hooded eyes. "That won't help us. Tell us how the two of you managed to escape without his help."

For the next half hour, she and Emily explained how they had managed to sneak away. When they told of their close call with one of the minions, Colin pressed Emily for answers. Do you think they obeyed you because they had been told to? Did he see Reba behind you? Tell me about the routine of the house. Was it completely quiet during the day? Did you get fed only at night or during the day? When did the coven awaken? She answered him as best as she could, but her ordeal in the house had left her unable to remember much, and frankly, she had been stuck in a tiny ill-lit room with no access except when called for by the Madame.

One final question. "Did you hear or see anything unusual when you were escaping? Any noise or strange portraits on the wall?" They couldn't answer to seeing any portraits as the hallways were too dark to see much and they kept their flashlights down and forward to help them avoid obstacles.

Things on the wall simply weren't important. "We did hear something though," Emily remembered. "Just as we made it to the cellar, we heard a loud

Eternal Diet — Wendy Wilson

bump and then something like a piano being knocked around. It sounded like a big piano too. We didn't wait around to see what it was."

Chapter Thirty

By the time he got Reba to accept that he wasn't going to go with her and Luc and was going to do some exploring on his own, Willie was ready to hit something over the head with his stake. Sometimes his friends could be so damn obstinate. Wasn't that the idea? He would look around while Reba found Emily? Did she think they would have the time to do both things together?

No, the only thing to do was split up, and each do part of the plan. The longer they stayed in the house, the more danger they were in. Plain fact was they had to split up to cover more ground. He secured the stake and hammer in his belt and began his search.

Carefully Willie pushed open the first door. It was full of closed coffins and very quiet. Which was as you'd expect in a room full of the sleeping dead. All of the coffins were simple boxes made of inexpensive wood with no decorations. They looked like the kind of caskets used for cremations instead of burial in soil. He wondered if they were chosen because they were

Eternal Diet   Wendy Wilson

the cheapest. They probably would be made of the cheapest and lightest wood, just perfect for burning. So many people were choosing cremation over traditional burial nowadays.

    The next room offered much the same. About six coffins lined up closely together. Each room after the first had its complement of coffins. It seems as if every room, from the dining room to billiard room had at least several coffins in it. By the time Willie had gone down the first hall, he had counted about twenty coffins. And he hadn't opened all the doors yet. A scuffling sound came from around the corner, and he dove back into the room he had just checked.

    He kept the door opened a crack and watched as one of the slaves shuffled past. It seemed to be looking for something, but it didn't open any doors. As the minion walked by into the dark and the sound of his passing diminished, Willie slowly opened the door and peeked out. Off in the distance, he could hear a faint noise. Not a shuffling sound but plinking noises like water into a sink. He decided to follow the sound.

    The wooden floor under his feet was fine cypress wood probably cut and planed from the surrounding swamp. A long time ago talented craftsmen who knew what they were doing had joined the planks together

Eternal Diet   *Wendy Wilson*

and after almost 175 years they didn't creak. A fact Willie appreciated more and more as he got closer to the source of the plinking noise. It no longer sounded so much like a faulty water faucet. Now it sounded more like someone repeatedly hitting the highest key on a piano keyboard. A faint memory stirred in the back of his mind. What did a piano mean? Something tickled his nose, and he sneezed. The plinking stopped.

And so did Willie. His foot froze in half step making his balance an exercise in acrobatics. He listened, his ears straining to hear the finest of vibrations. Silence. Wait. There it is was again. A tiny plinking. And now another note added, this one in harmony. Another and another and soon it was fingers flying over the keys like a swallow diving and dipping. Willie began to recognize the melody from a space back in his memory. But he had never played the piano. He had never played any instrument. So why did he know this complicated and profoundly expressive music?

The hallway began to spin. Vertigo spun Willie into the wall, and he leaned against it breathing great gasps of air. He knew where he had heard the music before. In his dream of terror and death. A voice he had known since the womb called out. "Come in, Mr. Willie. Don't stand outside. I've been waiting for you."

Eternal Diet   *Wendy Wilson*

His limbs moved of their own volition. Willie could no more control them then he could control the stars moving in the night sky. The door creaked open revealing a large curtained dark room, one that might have been called a music room in a more genteel era. Somehow Willie felt the word 'genteel' applied only to the room, not its current inhabitant. A shadow within a shadow stirred and stepped into his flashlight's beam.

"I've been waiting for you," the small-bodied woman said. "Come, sit down. Do not act the stranger Willie. You and I have met before." Again, Willie felt his limbs controlled by a power other than his own; a stool was at his feet, and he collapsed onto it. It was a struggle, but Willie reached for the stake and hammer and with fumbling fingers, tried to pull them from his belt. They kept slipping from his hands, which felt as huge as a plow horses' hooves, and he had as much ability to manipulate his fingers as the horse.

Madame laughed, her voice a melodious blend of silver bells and a brook babbling over mountain pebbles. With an undertone of fingernails scraping on a slate. "Oh, how I enjoy watching the living attempt to thwart my will. It is one of my few amusements in my long existence that I still enjoy" The voice changed to one of steel and iron. "Even so, your pathetic attempts do start to wear thin after so long. Can you not come up with something new?"

She placed one of her exquisitely enameled fingernails under Willies chin and skated it along his neck. Blood began to flow from the cut and Willie began to gag and cough. "Oh, do not be so over dramatic! It is merely one cut and not even a deep one. Nothing vital has been severed. We have only just begun.

Madame smiled, revealing her spiky white teeth, two of which were of outstanding sharpness. "It is rare that I have time alone with a living person. All of my people making such demands on my time! Why I barely have time to eat!" Slowly she walked around Willie who still could not move. Another quick slash on top of his scalp. He gasped again and felt the blood trickle down his forehead, being diverted by his eyebrows down to his cheeks.

"Now that I have time to play, I am going to go back to my roots, as you modern people say and use an ancient technique. It was normally reserved for heinous crimes, but for this lesson, I will use it for another reason. See if you can guess. This method is called Lingchi, but it goes by a more modern term I am sure you have heard of." She waited for an answer. "No? You don't know? Death by a Thousand Cuts.

You would not deny me some fun, would you? Even I need to be entertained." Willie's face blanched and he fought against the mental bindings that held him in place.

"In case you are familiar with the traditional form of Lingchi, don't worry. I will not cut off any of your limbs. I want you whole. Have you guessed why?"

"Because c...c..at plays with her m...mouse?"

"You disappoint me, Willie. Yes, some of it is the playful game of a cat and her quarry, but there is another reason. I have already hinted at it." She leaned in close and with a motion of her hand, Willie's pants were ripped apart. "I said I would not remove any of your 'limbs,' but I did not promise to not touch them."

He screamed. Pain ripped through his body as the most tender parts of a man's body were sliced from root to bud. Blood began to drip through his legs and onto the floor.

Madame released him enough to allow him to fall onto the floor curled around the center of his pain. She stood patiently looming over him. "You are a most remarkable man. You are intelligent but yet you cannot answer my question." Through gritted teeth, Willie asked her what her question was.

The pain began to lesson from burning hot coals to a lower flame. "I don't know why you are doing this! Cruelty is its own excuse."

"Cruelty? No! Motivation! Motivation is why I do this." She leaned in close, her bloody fingernail hovering over his eyeball. "You have to ask for it."

"Ask for....?" A revelation dawned in his eyes. He knew what he was supposed to ask for.

"No."

"No? I suppose I must continue our game then. At least you know the question now. See? I knew you were intelligent."

Her nails were very sharp. Before long the floor became slippery with blood. "You are wasting so much!" She shook her finger at Willie. "There are two ways for this to end. One; you ask for the change. Two; I change you by force."

Willie could feel his strength slipping. He needed to know one thing. Through the pain of what felt like a thousand cuts he gasped. "Why? Why me?"

"Why you? Because you interest me. You were the first in centuries to resist me in your dreams. You are a challenge." Her black eyes narrowed. "And I will have you, willing or not."

Willie reached deep into his soul and found courage. He stood up and roared. "NO!" And flung himself at her. She stepped aside, and he collided with the grand piano. A discordant clang of keys, hammers, and strings breaking apart rolled through the room as he clung to the frame and pulled himself up to face Madame. "Look what you have done, you stubborn fool! A priceless antique destroyed!"

The room grew darker, and Madame seemed to grow, her arms outstretched longer than human arms could be. Anger and blood thirst flashed in her eyes and clouds seemed to be gathering around her ever-enlarging body. Willie whimpered. This was it; he had fought as long and as hard as he could to give Reba and Emily time. He had lost, and Madame had won. Her body blotted out the ceiling. Her needle-sharp teeth filled his vision coming ever closer and closer until all he could sense was his death.

The remains of the piano became the sole thing holding Willie up as the visage of doom came nearer. His universe was her; the foul breath from between her red lips; the rasping of her tongue over sharpened fangs; the feel of her claws digging into his shoulders as she lowered her fangs to his neck. When fang met neck, Willie cried out. All he was and ever would be had come to an end. For a few moments, his sanity lingered long enough for him to try to hold onto the vision of his friends. The friends that were always there for him. Except now.

Eternity. That's how long it took. Millisecond. That's how fast it happened. Madame sucked his blood from his veins. The pain from the many cuts flared. Then she did something he didn't expect. She withdrew and bit her own wrist and held it to his lips. He struggled weakly, his strength leaving him quickly. His vision narrowed until it was pinpointed on Madame's face. A vicious smile grew on her lips. With a voice so smooth it could have been his own mother humming a melody she shushed him. "Don't fight. Drink, my little man. You know you want to. I am giving you Life Eternal. All your pain will be gone. Shhhh."

A drop of her blood slid into his mouth, and he swallowed. More flowed and again he swallowed. The pain from the cuts receded. He felt energy and vigor surge through his limbs, repairing all his wounds. He wanted more. And more. His hands grasped Madame's arms and pulled her towards him, digging his own teeth into the wound to draw the elixir deep into his body.

As his wounds healed, he felt a surge of lust and tried to push Madame over so he could dominate her as a man dominates a woman. She laughed and pushed him aside. "No, that is not going to happen. You have fully crossed over." She regarded him and gave another small laugh. "Well, almost fully."

Willie raised himself up onto his knees. "What do you mean, almost?"

"There is one more part of the ritual you have to pass through. It will happen very soon."

Simultaneous with her explanation, Willie felt a great pain rise up in his stomach. He glared at Madame. "You lied! You have killed me!"

Madame smiled. "That is one way of saying it." And sat back to witness his becoming.

Chapter Thirty -One

Later that night, Colin had insisted Reba take Emily to a motel. "Why can't we just go back to the boarding house?"

"If Willie has been turned." The girls cringed. "If he has been turned, as I believe he has, he knows where to find you. Do you really think he will remain your friend after someone as cruel and strong as Madame has control of him?"

"But Gwen is ok! She isn't trying to hurt us."

"Some of us remember our humanity. Blood drinkers like Madame do not and the creatures she creates cannot. I do not know what her purpose or plan was to kidnap Emily or trick Willie into being cornered, but I suspect it is to lure me into her sphere again.

"Take her to a motel, let neither of us know where, and we will meet again later tonight. This time at the ferry on Canal Street. We will find you." Before the women could open their mouth to replay the two vampires had vanished into the night.

"Guess we go find a motel." "There's a few things at the room I have to collect before though." They walked away into the dark to get those things unaware that a pair of eyes followed every step.

Emily turned to Colin. "Why did we leave them? Shouldn't we stay and help!"

"In a few hours. First, we have some hunting to do. You did say you were hungry earlier, didn't you?" This time when he smiled the tips of his razor-sharp incisors poked out just below his upper lip. "I have a plan. Tonight you will feast."

"But won't that..."

"Exactly. Let us hunt."

For the first time since she had been changed, Colin took Gwen to the part of Lake Pontchartrain that they had visited on her early hunts. He knew her memories would fuel her hunger. The pickings for vampires who preyed almost exclusively on the underside of society were excellent in the area. "I remember this place! I had my first sugar overdose here!" Gwen happily declared.

"Shhh. No need to announce our presence. Come follow me." He led her down a particularly rundown alley that dead-ended in a dilapidated warehouse abandoned after Gloria. The doors hung on their hinges, and not one window had a complete pane of glass. Inside, they could hear voices.

"Hey man, this ain't the best place to do this. It's just the sorta place the cops would be looking at."

"You gotta better place to unload the cargo? It ain't as if we can hide them in our backpacks to keep 'em quiet, now is it? Chill, bro. We'll get them moved soon. It ain't as if there's no demand for them!" He chuckled at his witticism.

This intrigued the two hidden listeners, and they looked at each other in puzzlement. What was too big to hide easily that would also need to be kept quiet? Something alive. The dots were easy to connect. Living cargo...in demand...cops were aware of the trafficking of such contraband...and whatever noise they made could be identified as not belonging in the area. Human trafficking. Probably women.

Gwen's heart began to race. Colin shushed her again and pointed to the dock. Six big guys emerged from behind a cargo container leading a line of stumbling, drugged women ranging in age from mid-twenties down to early teens off of a luxury yacht moored in front of the warehouse. It flew the Cayman Island flag even though the name of the boat was distinctly American: American Pride. Some rich folks not only ditching paying taxes but using human flesh to boost their financial portfolio's ready cash.

"Wait until they are inside." Colin directed when he felt Gwen tense up... "If we attack now the three outside will run."

Gwen nodded. "And if we wait until they are all inside...gotcha."

Colin pointed to the roof and himself. "Wait for my signal." Gwen nodded again, and Colin leapt up and disappeared into the night sky. A faint bump told her he was on the roof. *I wonder what the signal is.* She found out when a loud crash of glass blasted from the roof and yells and screams erupted from inside. Gwen raced to the door just as it was pushed out by one of the four guides.

She kicked him back inside. "Not so fast, you're not going anywhere!"

Gwen took a moment to pull the latch and bend it so bad it couldn't be pushed back and turned to face the runner laying on his back looking at her and the lock and then back again to her. "What? Did you think I was gonna let you just run out?" They guy's look of astonishment turned to terror when she dropped her fangs. "Thanks for laying down. It makes it so much easier."

She laughed as the man scrambled backwards like a crab to escape. Just before she dropped to tear at his throat, she kicked the guy in the nuts. For fun. And for the women. His scream of fear and pain tasted so good.

Her next meal offered himself to her by trying to shoot her with his pistol. When the bullet passed through her shoulder and hit the guy on the floor, she jumped up. "Look what you did, you idiot! You killed him! And. I. Wasn't. Finished!" Well, one meal interrupted, another one standing rooted to the floor right in front of her. With breakneck speed, she grabbed his throat and sunk in her fangs before he had a chance to open his mouth.

The hot blood, like salty sweet syrup, poured into Gwen's mouth. Gulping at the nectar flowed like silk down her throat she began to feel a familiar twinge down below and in her nipples. She sucked deep and swallowed hard. Before she could come to a finish, the heart started to skip. "No more or its death." She recited like a schoolgirl remembering a lesson. Tossing the second thug aside she watched as he collapsed onto the concrete floor, gave a few twitches and then lay still.

Now more than her thirst was awake. She needed more to satisfy her needs. In the semi-lit darkness of the huge building, she could see Colin finishing up and wiping his mouth. He grinned a bloody smile and nodded at what she thought were dead bodies. "I saved these for you. Amazing how easy it is to knock one of them out! They are alive, waiting for you. I cannot guarantee their consciousness, however." He made one of his rare grand gestures for her to indulge as one of the thugs stirred. "Ah! Here is one coming around to invite you to dinner."

Not one to refuse largesse when it is offered, Gwen grabbed the semi-conscience man and shook him until his eyes popped open. They rolled around and finally focused on Gwen. And widened until the blue-flecked green iris was entirely surrounded by white. "No...no...no!"

Gwen nodded. "Yes...yes ...yes...But I'm gonna take a little bit of time with you."

Colin cleared his throat. "That's not a good idea. The prisoners all ran out earlier. There is no telling how long it will take for them to find the authorities. And then they will swarm this place." He did a little 'I'm sorry' shrug. "You don't have time to indulge in foreplay. We must be gone before they get here."

"Damn it, Colin! Why didn't you stop them?"

"Like you, I was distracted. Come, hurry up and we can continue with our job tonight knowing we helped those poor women." Gwen mumbled and bit and drank as quickly as she could. By the fourth one she could feel her clothes pinching and her shorts riding up her thighs. Still, it had been too long a time between full meals, and she enjoyed this one. At least she had on comfortable shoes. And it was a good thing her shoes were good for running because before she had finished with the last one, the two of them were speeding their way down the alleyway and into the tourist part of town away from the police.

Gwen pulled Colin out of her run before they made it to the appointed rendezvous. "Now are you gonna tell me why you wanted me to indulge to the point of getting fat? Even though it doesn't last long, it's still a pain in the neck, and the ass...and the ankles... Better be a good reason to make me go through this."

"Oh, there is." His voice went into teacher mode. "Of all the things we are, what is the one thing that vampires are NOT?" Gwen looked at him as if he'd gone crazy. Her head cocked left and right trying to figure out the one thing that did NOT describe vampires. Colin gave her a hint. "It's what brought you here."

She knew. "No vampire is fat! Every fucking blood drinker is an Adonis or Aphrodite!" She went to high five Colin, but he just looked at her as if her enthusiasm was carrying her away. "Ok, so no high five. But how is it gonna work?"

Colin disappeared for a moment, and when he came back, he handed her a bundle of clothes. "These should fit you. Maybe we should cache some all over the city." Gwen frowned at him, and they walked the remaining mile or so to their pre-arranged meeting,

Colin outlined his plan. "One of the ways we recognize each other is by our outward form. Because none of us are fat, we usually do not look beyond that when we suspect others of our kind are in the area. It is a weakness I believe we can exploit. Ah, your friends are over there. Let's go join them." The closer they got to the two women the clearer it became that they were agitated about something. "I wonder what's got them freaked out."

Reba jumped up when she saw the two vampires approaching. "You won't believe it! We went back to the room..."

Colin interrupted them. "You went back to the room? After I told you to get a motel room?"

His anger set Reba off her excitement a little. "Yeah, we had some stuff we needed to pick up. What's the problem?" Colin waved for her to continue her story. "Well, we went back to the room, and we both had a funny feeling. Right, Em?" Emily nodded quickly.

"It felt like someone was watching us."

"And still you went to the room."

Colin shook his head. "Have you learned nothing? But it appears as if nothing bad happened to you. Please go on."

"I'm trying to, but you keep interrupting! So, again… if felt as if someone was watching us, so we ducked down behind some huge bushes and waited. See? We were careful. Nothing happened so we went up to the room and got our stuff together."

Emily couldn't restrain herself. "He was there!"

It was Gwen's time to chime in though she had an idea who the 'he' was. "Who was there?"

"Willie!" Both yelled in unison.

When neither Gwen nor Colin burst into frantic questions, they realized this was not a huge surprise for them. Colin hung his head and asked them; "Why do you think I told you to go somewhere else? Willie knows where you are staying. You are unfinished business that he must tidy up to keep his new life a secret. How did you escape?"

"That's just it! He didn't try to attack us. He wants to talk to you two. Or at least Gwen." Emily looked at her sister. "He did seem to want to talk to you the most. There was another, ah, person, with him he said. He had ducked him to come to us. He couldn't stay long; just enough to tell us to be at the bar at 1:00."

"Then we must hurry if we are to be ready." With that, Colin spun on his heel and sped off into the night leaving the three women behind.

"Ready with what? Where's he going?"

"Dunno. Be back soon." And then Gwen was gone too.

"Wait" Gwen called. "Where are we going?" They ran on for a few more blocks and stopped in front of an all-purpose store; one of those stores that sold everything from veggies to high tech and everything in between.

"Yes, this one will have what we need." Colin walked in through the automatic doors. He turned around to see if Gwen was following him.

"What do we need in here?"

"Do you still have your wallet?"

"What?" Gwen patted her shorts. Putting her wallet in her pocket was a habit she had found difficult to break, even when wearing a dress, she still carried it in a small bag. No reason for it really, just old habits die hard.

"Yeah, I have it. Why?"

"There are a few things we need to get to be ready for tonight. Where would we find receptacles to carry gasoline? And a long-bladed knife as well." This late at night there weren't as many shoppers as during the day, but there were still enough for Gwen and Colin to have to weave in and out of traffic.

At one point, Colin stopped dead, staring at a stringy man with a rainbow mullet and piercings up and down his face, pick up a baby doll and seriously examine the quality of the toy.

"C'mon, Colin. There's weirdos all over the place, you should know that by now."

The auto department had the gasoline cans they wanted. When they asked about the hunting knives, the clerk led them to the usual 7" to 8" blades. Clearly not satisfied, Colin explained he wanted a longer blade. He mimicked swinging a sword. "We need something longer, much longer."

The clerk was getting a little nervous at these two obviously non-outdoor types getting gas cans and large bladed knives. Gwen jumped in. "We need these to clear some property, you see." She chortled. "You must think us strange; we obviously don't do our own garden work! We told our gardener that we would have these ready for him when he showed up in the morning. We came now because you see, we're night people."

She shook her head and leaned across the counter into the clerk. "We don't do days well at all." He stared at her long enough until she wondered if she had wiped her lips and teeth clean of blood. But the clerk figured a sale was a sale and her story made sense. He rang up their purchases. On the way out Gwen crowed. "Yup! You need me. I'm just surprised my card is still good!"

A quick stop at a gas station and they were ready. Reba and Emily were still at the Ferry entrance, but they had apparently anticipated tonight's activity and were dressed for action. Both wore sneakers and tee shirts as well as durable material pants. "Excellent, you are ready for an active night." Colin gathered them close and told them what was going to happen.

The two pairs parted and each started their part of the operation. Reba and Emily each lifted one of the full gas cans and started walking out of town to find a close but hidden spot in the swamp by the mansion. There they were to wait for the signal. By the time they had found the place Gwen had told them to hide in they were glad of the long pants and sleeves; the mosquitos were brutal even with bug spray. "At this rate, we won't have to worry about vampires,"

Eternal Diet   *Wendy Wilson*

Reba whispered as she pulled a cap down over her ears. "These little bloodsuckers will have gotten all of our blood!"

Chapter Thirty-Two

Antoine, one of Madame's cohorts was tired of babysitting this new fledgling. It was quite boring to have to watch over a newly made vampire and make sure he didn't bring attention onto them because of his enthusiastic but clumsy hunting. And he was halfway ready to let this one feed until the victim's heart failed. Let him go down with the meal. Why couldn't one of the others do it? Didn't the maker have the responsibility of teaching the made one? Antoine's annoyance was evident in every gesture and conversation he had with Willie. His anger was directed at the all-powerful and imperious Madame, but he could not dare act on it, so he let it out on Willie.

Willie knew Antoine was just barely tolerating him, and that was fine. Let him get sloppy. Antoine pushed past him and snapped his fingers. "We're going to the bar now."

"But I haven't finished! I need more!"

"Get someone at the bar to nursemaid you, I am finished!" Antoine was about to leave Willie on his own when a faint scent caught his attention. He sniffed. He stepped into the street and sniffed again. There it was! The scent of another vampire! But the only biped he could see was a waddling fat woman strolling down the street. It couldn't possibly be her. Maybe it was the scent of the vampires in the bar he smelled. Whatever it was, he knew it couldn't be that overweight, dowdy woman. He shook his head and went into the bar.

Willie could sense a vampire coming. But something was wrong with this one; her body silhouette was not slim and straight but fat and lumpy. Still, there was something strangely familiar about the figure approaching him. Like a firecracker exploding in his head, he realized who it was. "Gwen!"

"Shhhh. Don't make a noise. We don't want your friends in there to hear us. What did you want to talk to me about?"

He stood there shaking his head. "Reba and Emily probably told you what happened to me."

"Yeah, they said. I'm so sorry Willie. I got you into this. It's all my fault. You should have stayed home."

"You're a friend Gwen, and we had to find out what happened to you. We maybe didn't know what was going on at first but, well, now I know first-hand."

Eternal Diet *Wendy Wilson*

He looked at her head to foot. "I thought vampires were all gorgeous and thin but look…"

"Yeah, look at me, Willie. I'm not thin. I'm fat. It comes and goes. Get over it."

Willie was stunned. But then he remembered why he wanted to talk to her. "Gwen, you've got to get out of New Orleans. There's danger here …a very old and evil vampire is going to take over, and any vampire who stands in her way will be obliterated. I mean it! She's been building an army! I saw all the caskets in the mansion…she's almost ready."

"Then it's a good thing we have a plan." Gwen grinned. And she explained to Willie the plan Colin had concocted, including his part.

Before he had a chance to answer, the door to the bar opened, and Antoine stepped out. He hesitated at seeing Willie next to a fat woman and decided to watch the show. Willie grabbed Gwen by the neck and drew her against him. Lowering his teeth to her neck, he whispered for her to scream and pretend to go limp.

"I know what to do," Gwen whispered back and then took a breath and started to scream. Willie burying his mouth in her neck cut her off, and as she slid to the sidewalk, he followed her down.

Eternal Diet   *Wendy Wilson*

For a moment, just a moment but still...Gwen felt Willie wasn't quite acting. He seemed to be fighting himself, and she had a flash of fear, and suddenly her struggles weren't all pretend.

Antoine was disgusted. "Don't you know better than to feed right out in the open? Get her back into the alley you idiot!" He contemplated the pair. "At least you got yourself a fat one. She should top you off quite nicely. Hurry up. It's time to go." He turned with a flourish and disappeared again, this time out of town and towards the swamp.

Gwen struggled weakly as she was dragged off into a dark corner. Just because he hadn't actually broken her skin with his teeth did not calm her fear, but her friend's safety depended on the others believing he was with them and she wasn't sure if there were any more watchers at the door...

She allowed him to drag her out of sight and then threw Willie off of her and jumped up. He was a little bit slow in releasing her. His eyes grew foggy, and he licked his bared lips. The hunger threatened. Instinctively she crouched. He was stronger, but she had experience. They were a match if it came to battle.

It couldn't be allowed to happen. "Willie!" She hissed. "Get a hold of yourself! We're friends. Don't let the hunger take over your good sense." They circled each other; sizing the other up for weakness while Gwen continued to speak softly and gently about how they were good friends. Slowly the foggy look faded and her friend stood before her again. Gwen let out a sigh of relief. "You had me scared for a hot minute. You know what to do, right?"

"Yes, I got it. Don't worry about me."

When Gwen joined up with Colin later, she was still a bit shaken by her encounter with Willie. "He was ready to tear me to pieces. And I gotta say I was ready to do the same to him. Why? We're friends, have been for years."

"You no longer have friends. You have prey and enemies. Although occasionally enemies can band together to become a coven if there is a strong enough leader to hold them in check."

"But what about you? You're not an enemy. And I don't want to drink your blood."

Colin's left eyebrow raised while he stood with crossed arms. "Are you sure you wouldn't welcome a sip from my veins?" Hunger suddenly blossomed in her, and she bared her teeth. He saw the look and nodded. "Of course; you are a blood drinker. To drink the blood of another vampire is to gain much of their strength, just as drinking the blood of a drunk victim makes you giddy. I am neither prey nor enemy, I am your maker. That is a totally different situation. Now, put your fangs away and listen." Without even realizing she had done it, Gwen's fangs retracted and the desire to drink faded.

There was a full moon that night. Which was a good thing because Reba and Emily were able to watch for any movement in the swamp. They could hear vampires traveling in the distance as they entered and left the mansion with no inkling spies were so close. Colin had shared a secret that vampires have trouble sensing humans when there are great amounts of animal life surrounding them. Especially if they stayed perfectly still. And mosquitoes qualified as animal life, so they were safe for now. "I'm gonna take a bath in calamine lotion for the next three days, and then I'm gonna drink an entire bottle of booze and sleep for the next three!"

"You and me both, sister." Reba agreed. They jumped when they heard the quiet steps of two beings right behind them.

"Geez Gwen! Scare a person to death, why don't ya!" Emily whispered with a whoosh of air. Then she realized what she had just said and who she had said it to. "Oops, sorry Gwen. I didn't mean anything by that."

Gwen gave her sister a swat on the arm. "No need to apologize Sis." She looked around the area. "Seen anything interesting?"

"By interesting do you mean vampires? Yes. They've been going in and out all night. Other than that, it's' just us and our mosquito buddies." She smashed one that had landed on her knuckle and inspected the ooze of blood. "Is everything ready? When do you want us to go?"

"Everything's in place. Willie's on board. You have the cans and Colin and I..." She nodded in the direction on the other side of the two women. They jumped; he hadn't been there a moment before. "...we're ready to start the distraction. Just wait for it."

"What exactly is the signal?" Reba wanted to know.

"Don't worry. You'll know it when it happens. You just be ready to run to the house." The vampires slid silently into the darkness of the swamp.

Emily looked at Reba. "You ready?" "Ready as I'll ever be."

Chapter Thirty -Three

Colin and Gwen wended their way through the cypress trees until they stood at the beginning of the little hillock the mansion stood on. "What do we do now, Colin?"

"We, do nothing. I, do it from here. You go back to help Reba and Emily in their task."

"What?!? No!" Gwen hissed as quietly as she could, but her surprise amplified her voice into a cry.

Colin put his hand over her mouth and scanned the area for sentinels. "Shh. You must go now. It's time. You know what you need to survive, and you have held to your part of our bargain. Time for us to part."

Anguish filled her as Gwen tried to understand what her mentor and maker was saying. "But you're gonna come back! We don't have to...." The look on Colin's face cut short her plea. She swallowed hard and asked with a slightly lower tone. "What are you going to do?"

"I'm going to finish something I should have finished long ago." Colin looked at the mansion with a fury he rarely gave vent to. Gwen was glad she wasn't on the receiving end of that glare. "Goodbye." And he was gone, melted into the shadows as if he didn't exist.

On the way back to where her friends were hiding Gwen had to hide several times from members of the coven returning home in time for the dawn. Good thing there were too many vampires in the area for her one scent to be remarkable. But even so, she had a few close calls with vampires stopping close to her and sniffing. A vampire's sense of scent can be confused by the smell of fresh and decaying flora, and she escaped undiscovered.

Her friends were where she had left them waiting for the signal. They were worried they wouldn't know what it was and when Gwen tapped them on the back, they almost took off running with the cans of gasoline. "No, wait!" she whispered. "It's me, Gwen. I came back to help you guys."

"Where's Colin?"

Suddenly a voice roared out in the darkness. "Madame Li of Chang'an! Hear me and heed my words. I have come to stop you. I have come to free your slaves. I have come to kill you."

Gwen stared sadly at the direction of the voice. "I think that's him giving us our signal."

"Madame Li, come out and face me. One on one." Gwen crept as close as she dared. She had to at least witness Colin's action; if only to believe it herself. Where he had hidden it while traveling to the mansion, Gwen couldn't begin to guess, but he had on a real live cloak, one that a highwayman might choose. Completely black with shiny redlining it covered him from neck to just above the calf-high riding boots he wore and swirled around in a lighter than air flight.

The boots were straight out of central casting costume, shiny dark brown leather with folded over tops. Gwen squinted and could see two thin bulges running down his back beneath the cape. "So that's why he wanted them!"

As Colin threw down his challenge members of the coven began to circle around him, unsure of what their mistress would want. Colin never took his eyes off of the mansion. It was as if the vampires revolving around him were unworthy of notice. "Madame Li, you know who it is that…" A vassal of Madame's rushed at him. Colin's hand flashed and caught it and crushed its throat… "…challenges you." He tossed the lackey at the feet of the other vampires. It lay there choking and gasping. The others stepped back.

More and more of Madame's lackeys joined as word had gone out to them all about the challenge, but none had the courage to test the speed of Colin's hand. They waited for their mistress to show them what to do. Colin gave voice again. "Will you hide behind your lackeys? Or do you want me to come look for you as you cower in your hiding place?" The vampires encircling Colin were beginning to look anxious. Many had their faces turned to the mansion, waiting for her to come out and take care of this raucous man.

A small cheer rose up as a small form dressed head to toe in silk emerged from the shadows of the doorway. She was dressed in a deep red silk dress. Over her dress was a cream jacket with loose flowing sleeves. This was tied with a length of silk wrapped around her middle. In her hands, she carried a 12-inch fan painted with chrysanthemums and lotus flowers. On her head, her coal black hair was piled high amid elaborate hairpins and flower ornaments.

"I see you have dressed up for the occasion, Madame." Colin gave a formal bow and sweeping his hand low he continued. "You do me honor."

Madame's eyes narrowed further, and a snarl lifted her lips. "The honor is not for you, My Lord." She lifted her chin high. "I do honor to my ancestors. But honoring family is something you are unfamiliar with Colin Selby!"

"How I honor my family is my business. How I vanquish you is a matter between you and I."

Madame hissed at him, her face a rictus of hate. "I grant you single combat." She opened her steel ribbed fan and flung herself at him.

Reba could feel Gwen quivering beside her. She knew Gwen well enough to know she was only a hair away from racing away to stand beside her maker. Reba also knew that was the last thing Colin wanted her to do. It wouldn't help and might get her, well maybe not killed, Reba didn't know what might happen, but she was sure it would be a disaster for them all for Gwen to run out there right now.

Tentatively, Reba placed her hand on Gwen's rigid shoulder. "You can't go…" Both she and Emily fell back when Gwen spun around on them and growled, revealing her very sharp and very pointed teeth.

This time Emily tried. A sister might be the better choice for this. "Gwen, you can't…"

"Don't you try to tell me what I can't do! I am immortal! And I can do what I like!" She stood up and towered over the pair. Emily and Reba both were numbed into silence. Gwen had seemed to grow twice her height, looking over them with her lips drawn back into a snarl. Suddenly she collapsed onto the bit of dry ground. "I want to help him; I NEED to help him."

"Then come and help us carry out his plan. He wouldn't want you to fail him in this. Please."

The trio gathered the gas cans, and under cover of Colin's calling his challenges to Madame, they were able to cross the open yard and dive into the cover of the wall of the house. It blocked them from sight, but they could hear all that was going on. "Willie is supposed to be waiting for us to open the door. Where is he? Wasn't he supposed to be here by now?"

"Don't worry, Em. I talked to him myself not long ago. He knows what he's supposed to do." They hunkered down, hoping none of the blood drinkers watching Colin decided to do a check on the perimeter. Just as the vampires gave a huge cheer and they could hear Colin compliment Madame on her attire the secret door slid open and Willie pulled them in.

"Did you bring everything?"

"Yes," Reba answered. "Got the cans here and Em has the lighters. Where should we place them?" Willie indicated the wooden beams central to the house and dry enough to carry the flames up into the building itself, and they set the cans around the beams.

"We need some tinder; the beams won't just go up fast."

So the group searched the various cages and came up with enough old rags and straw to work as tinder. At last, the set up was complete. Gwen took a can of butane fire starter and squirted out a liquid fuse long enough to reach the door. "There. We're ready. Only one problem. Who's gonna light the fuse?"

"I will." Said a voice from the door. It was Luc. "Colin asked if I would be willing to come back and help."

Emily as amazed. "He found you?"

"No, I thought about what you'd said. I couldn't just pretend I wasn't involved, so I found him. I can maybe even get the others to help."

"The other slaves? They would do that?"

Luc shrugged. "I really dunno. But I do know they used to take orders. And I'm enough like'em for'em to listen to me."

It all sounded set. The plan should work. Reba and Emily turned to go. "C'mon, let's go." Willie didn't move. Gwen echoed them. "You're coming with us now Willie." She reached for his arm; he drew back. "What's wrong? You can't stay here! This place is gonna be a firetrap soon. You'll die." She motioned insistently. "Come. Now."

He shook his head. "I can't go. I have to be here when they all come back into sleep. I don't think any noticed me slipping away, but if I am not in the house before dawn, they will come looking for me."

"Don't be silly, Willie." Reba urged. "You'd be cutting it very close if you stayed until dawn. You have to come with us and hope they don't notice you not being there."

Gwen understood. "He isn't expecting to get away, Reba."

"What! Don't be ridiculous! Of course, he's getting away. With us. Right now." She grabbed again at Willies arm.

He grabbed hers instead and peered deeply into her eyes. "Antoine will look for me. He doesn't like me. He has made it his job to keep me in line. He WILL look for me. And he will search all over the house." His eyes indicated upwards and then back to room they were in. "Upstairs and downstairs."

Reba blanched. "And he will find the gas cans." She gave up on changing Willie's mind. A hug was all she had left to give him. All that any of them had to give. They broke the hug and Gwen whispered in Willie's ear. "If you can get out. We'll be at the boarding house." He nodded, unable to speak. The friends parted knowing the chances of ever seeing each other again were abysmally slim.

Willie rejoined the scene in front of the mansion just in time to witness the start of the battle between these two most powerful vampires. Everyone's attention was riveted on their mistress who had appeared on the lawn. Challenge had been set and accepted. The fight began.

Colin faced the fury that flew at him. Her rage inflamed her voice as she screamed curses at him. A foot away from him she twisted to his left and raked his face with her adamantine fan. Colin dropped to the ground and swung his foot out to trip her. She stumbled, and he followed through with a vicious kick to her knee. She cried out and dropped to one knee. Her hands a blur of color and steel blocking any chance of follow through. They rose to their feet and stepped back, breathing hard; both in pain and both assessing the other.

A little more cautious this time, they circled like two boxers, feinting left and right searching for their opponent's weakness. Colin eyed the fan; it was dangerous in its own right, and in Madame's hands it was a lethal weapon.

Madame saw the opening and struck with a flurry of kicks to Colin's head. One connected and with a grunt of surprise blood flew from his mouth, spattering the surrounding onlookers who now, having literally tasted blood were becoming aroused. Any more and Colin knew they would not be restrained.

"Madame Li! This is Single Combat! Take your creatures away. This is between you and me!"

With heaving breath, Madame commanded her army to leave. "Leave us! Dawn approaches. I will take care of this ...this..." She examined Colin with a haughty sneer. "I will take care of this interloper into our reign. Go!" She screamed at them. With visible reluctance, the crowd around them dispersed. Willie caught Colin's eye and gave a small nod. The plan was going forward.

Once again, the two circled each other. "It is still not too late to join with me, Colin. I can overlook your earlier desertion if you join with me now. You have my blood in you. My ancient bloodline is powerful, more powerful with each passing year. Together nothing can stand in our way."

Colin snorted a laugh and spread his arms to encompass the building and swamp around them. "This? This could be mine? All of this? An abandoned house in the middle of nowhere and some sycophants?" His voice became sorrowful. "There was a time I might have joined with you; that time is gone.

Your time is gone. You never believed that you had to learn, had to grow to survive. Your hubris makes you vulnerable. And now it will take you down."

All the time Colin was speaking he was watching as Madame's coven retreated into the house, making sure none stayed behind to help her. When the door, at last, closed he put his full attention back onto his adversary. Just in time. Madame Li dove at him and shoved her shoulder against his body and as he twisted to regain balance she struck again with the fan, ripping a grouping of stripes along his cape deep enough to score his leg.

Colin roared and fell away from her strike. He staggered and slipped in the growing splotches of blood. Madame did not waste the chance. She flipped and ran at Colin as he panted in exhaustion. Her hands raised the fan for one more brutal slash. A flash of pain in her wrist and the fan was gone. No time to search for it, she roared in anger at his deception. He wasn't as tired as he looked. His charge took her by surprise.

Chapter Thirty -Four

Willie watched through the window as long as he could, but fatigue overcame him. He was amongst the youngest of the vampires, so he was one of the first to seek his casket, leaving the more senior ones to witness the battle. A pretty girl with a ponytail was right behind him.

It didn't matter who won, the trap had been set, and none of them were getting out. He didn't feel very noble as he walked the hallway, he wanted to scream and cry and run out to escape the coming devastation.

It was only because of drawing deep down into his friendship with Reba and Gwen and Emily too that he knew he had to do this. As he lowered the casket lid, he saw one of the minions come into the room. The look on its face wasn't as blank as it should have been. It even winked at Willie as he fell into sleep.

***

Luc kept asking "Now?" and kept getting "Not yet, the sun's not up." from the others. His nervousness was wearing on Reba who finally took the lighter from him to stop his incessant flicking. "We have to wait. Shut up, or they'll hear us, and then that's it. We're done. Right, Gwen?"

"Gwen?"

"I...I...I've gotta...go now. Sleep." Gwen stumbled away towards the city.

"I hope she didn't leave it too late." Reba muttered. Hunkered down behind some bushes close to the house, they sat and waited for the sun to rise. Never had they seen a sun take longer to rise than the one on that morning.

The battle carried on, seemingly endless, time to end it. Colin charged. Just as he was about to impact Madame, he veered off; his cloak billowing behind him, blinding her. A quick deep jab to her back and he knew he had damaged the viscera within. Her body flew into the stone wall, knocking a few stones away. He danced away just out of reach as she turned to find him. Not as fast as before, he noted. The impact against the wall had destroyed her knee.

Her speed may have lessened but not her rage. Blood engorged her eyes, and red blotches started to spread across her ivory complexion. She raised an unearthly howl and swung her fists wildly. Good, Colin thought, an enraged and wounded adversary is a reckless one.

Eternal Diet *Wendy Wilson*

He danced around her like Ali with the butterfly, jabbing and kicking, at times connecting with vital areas. Madame's fury rose, not in centuries had anyone dared challenge her! This was outrageous! She ruled! A wicked kick to her leg brought her to her knee again. It was taking longer to rise from each blow.

Another unearthly roar and she launched herself at his head. Her hands grabbed to rip his throat out. She wanted to tear him to pieces. She wanted to bathe in his blood as it flowed from his skin. Colin's arms were longer, his fingers wrapped around her throat before hers managed to grip tightly to his. They stood locked together, arm's length apart, both silent now in their hunger to annihilate the other. Veins bulged with stolen blood and began to leak. Both of their faces dripped blood into their eyes.

Colin began to spin. He had the better reach, and her arms fell away. He spun her by her neck until her feet lifted off the ground. He spun at an unearthly speed until both were a blur of black, red and cream. And then he pushed her away from him. She flew across the lawn and smacked into a tree. There was a loud crunch, and she collapsed like an unstrung marionette onto the roots.

"You don't kill a vampire by breaking their bones! Did you learn nothing from your time with me?" She struggled to rise, but even a strong vampire can't recover quickly enough from broken bones to respond to the speed that Colin came to her at.

He towered over her and raised both his hands to the collar of his cape. "I learned much from you, Madame, including what will kill us." His arms lifted from his collar as he drew out the two machete blades from their sheaths. Madame's eyes bulged, this time not in rage but fear. Again she tried to force her bones to obey. Again they refused to lift her off her knees. Colin crossed the razor-edged blades against her throat. And pulled.

Emily and Reba both gasped and hugged each other when they saw Madame's severed head fall to the ground. The body quivered, and then blood exploded into the air; a roman candle of blackish red viscous fluid covering everything within reach. They watched in horror as the body shrunk, drawn into itself and fell to join the severed head in the sodden pool of blood.

Colin turned to face the house, his cape dripping blood, his face a contorted gory, demonic mask. He saw Emily and Reba still there. And realized he was hungry after the fight. His feet began to move towards the girls before he could gain control. He stopped halfway; conflict evident as his human soul sense clashed with the base sense of the vampire he was. "GO! Get away!" He yelled in agonizing dread.

Like a deer in the headlights of an oncoming diesel, the girls stood rooted, too overcome with the gruesome scene to react. Colin's fists clenched, his limbs tightened, and he lifted his head to the heavens and let out a long reverberating howl. When he fell silent, he was in control again. "Go, get away and don't come back." His composed voice jolted the girls into action, and they ran away to find safety. If such a thing existed in the world they had entered.

Chapter Thirty-Five

Luc was waiting for Colin at the secret door. "I din't know if you were gonna make it."

"Neither did I, Luc. That's why I asked for your help. Are you still willing?"

"Yep. Got the slaveys finishing up, no!. None of those vampires will get out." He gestured to the front door as dozens of the pale gray clad slaves filed by. Some were carrying hammers and all were more animated than Colin had ever seen them. "Everyone out?"

They nodded and Colin turned to Luc with the lighter. "Do you want to do the honors?"

Luc grinned and flicked the lighter. "Yep, got it all set." He went down the steps as everyone else backed away from the house.

They waited at the edge of the lawn by the stonewall waiting for Luc. The sun continued to rise. The minions gathered together on one side of the property, leaving Colin by himself. Then a wisp of a scent of smoke drifted out of the building. The fire was going strong. Colin could leave and go to his rest.

Eternal Diet — Wendy Wilson

Even for a vampire as old and powerful as he was, he was still subject to the sun cycle. The sun would be free of the horizon in minutes. He had to leave to survive. What he had condemned those creatures in the house to would be on his conscience forever. Watching their torment was more than he could bear to do. He left to join Gwen in their refuge.

The flames began to lick at the window panes. Inside the building the heat was growing intense. Smoke choked the hallways and rooms. In the bottom floor the wooden railings and heavy beams were totally engulfed, flames climbed the stairs and burst into the halls. They met wooden moldings and floorboards saturated with decades of polishing oil and ran along as if the flames were in a race. Within minutes the entire main floor was engulfed. Solid wood doors were no obstacle for the blaze. They licked at the caskets piled in the rooms, quickly enveloped the wood and the sleepers within. Pounding sounds came from the caskets as the screaming occupants fought to escape only to fall back into ash.

The fire traveled down to the room where Madame held her audiences. There it found particularly fine wood and ivory to feed its appetite. For a brief time the room was as well-lit as if for a fancy ball awaiting the musicians and dancers to arrive.

Eternal Diet — Wendy Wilson

A loud crash sounded as windows blew apart allowing air in to feed the ravenous inferno. Fire crept up the walls and danced across the ceiling, devouring everything in its path. To stand in its path was to be immolated in an instant.

Outside, the minions waited for Luc to arrive. They would not leave until everything was complete. They could hear the screams and tortured howls of the vampires trapped in their coffins as they burned. And stroked the smooth metal of their hammers as they nodded, satisfied at a job well done. Finally, Luc came up beside them. "Is everything done?" The minions nodded again in acknowledgement of the fulfillment of the pact they had made with him. They watched as the building of their torture was reduced to blackened and smoking ash. Luc turned to the ipso facto leader of the minions. "I'm hungry. Anyone bring marshmallows?"

Chapter Thirty-Six

By the time Reba and Emily finally woke the sun was on its descent. They had tried to stay awake and listen for any news of a great fire outside of the city but weariness won, and finally, they had to give in to the heat and stillness pressing on them. Hours later the faint stirring of slightly cooler air drifted in through the window. Long shadows stretched across the floor. Emily woke first and stretched and yawned. Reba lay on her cot, slight snores issuing from her open mouth.

Emily padded over and gave her a shake. "Hey, Reba. We fell asleep. We gotta get up."

"Huh...what?" A not quite awake Reba also sat up and stretched. "Yeah, lets' go."

Without a better plan, and since they didn't know where Gwen and Colin went to ground, the two women decided to go to the mansion. It was a few hours before sunset. Madame was no longer a threat but what about the others? When they had left, there was no fire or any sign of Luc. What if he'd been caught? Was all their effort for nothing? They began the trek through the swamp to find the answers.

They hadn't gone far when several fire trucks passed them heading back to the city. Mud and muck from the swamp was caked over the rims and splashed up onto the sides. "Looks like these guys were on a call out in the swamp."

They looked at each other. "Dare we hope?" The prospect that the plan had come to fruition spurred their feet, and before too long they turned onto the deserted road to the mansion. Except it was far from deserted. Firefighters were rolling up hoses and packing equipment away. It was plain to see that a large conflagration had occurred. The mansion was a mere pile of blackened timber. Small spits of fire sprang up, but no one was messing with them.

Reba went up to the nearest firefighter. "Wow! What happened here?" He looked at her as if to say, 'what the hell are you doing here?' but he answered her instead.

"Someone set a fire, probably vagrants or such like. Got outta control and they split. Funny thing is it looks like somebody was storing a lot of nice wood in there." He shrugged, no telling what some folks will do…and returned to rolling up a hose. "Don't you go

Eternal Diet   *Wendy Wilson*

any closer, Miss! In fact, you shouldn't even be here. It's dangerous. Gonna be dark soon too."

"Don't worry, we just saw the fire trucks while we were out on a hike. Curiosity and all, you know." She waved and made as if to walk away.

It didn't take long for the trucks to get squared away and they left soon after. No one remained behind to investigate the blaze; no one claimed the property and as a derelict having it burn down was probably for the best. Reba and Emily found a spot out of sight and waited. Whatever survived would be showing up soon. The shadows got darker, and soon the only source of light was the moon struggling to get through the cypress tree branches hanging with Spanish moss and the burning embers of surviving flames.

The sounds of a swamp at night are rarely comforting. And to someone who knows what might be lurking in the murk, it was infinitely more disturbing. Reba and Emily jumped at every skreeek of an insect or whoosh of owl wings. The flames might be still low, and on this small hillock surrounded by swamp, it wasn't going to spread, but it did manage to throw up some scary shadows. Both women found themselves spinning around shining their flashlights into the dark at the slightest sound only to realize it was a frog or some other natural denizen of the swamp.

Emily squinted and shone her light at a particularly vocal cicada. At least the smoke from the fire was stopping the mosquitoes. "This is creeping me out. If nobody comes soon, we better go."

A male voice boomed from the darkness. "What, and leave us all alone?" Two screams tried to squeeze through the two throats but could only provide a tiny 'Squeek" as they leapt up.

Light from their flashlights dashed around in search of the owner of the voice. "Don't tease them, Colin. It's not right." It was Gwen!

"It serves them right." Colin's masculine voice answered. "They should not be here. What if we had been unsuccessful? What if Madame and her followers were still here?"

The light from the flashlight finally came to a stop in the area of the tree line where the voices had come from. Slowly the shadows coalesced into two forms, one male the other female as they stepped into the light. Both were utterly beautiful. Skin smooth and pale as a baby newly bathed with perfect hair highlighted by the remains of the fire. Each was dressed in immaculate expensive clothes that would be at home on a movie premiere red carpet. Gwen did a little spin. "You like it? We figured we should dress up to celebrate."

Hugs and greeting didn't last long, Reba and Emily could sense the two vampires were there only to make sure they were ok. It was evident they were anxious to get on with their nights work. The less Emily and Reba knew about it, the better for their peace of mind. Colin told the tale of what happened after the women had left. He left out the part of his sudden hunger and the difficulty he had controlling it. He told of finding Luc who had gotten the minion slaves to nail down the coffins to ensure no survivors.

Reba hung her head. "Even Willie? He helped us."

"I am afraid so, they only understood about trapping the sleepers. You must remember; it was his decision. Honor it."

Finally, it was time to part. Emily took Gwen aside and asked if there was anything she wanted her to tell the family. "Tell them I am happy and healthy. And beautiful." One last hug and they parted; Emily and Reba to pack and catch a plane home and Gwen and Colin to melt into the New Orleans shadows and hunt.

"Colin, do you think maybe we can go somewhere else? I miss my mountains."

"I don't see why not. The town has lost its allure for me as well."

None of them were aware of the eyes that watched their reunion and parting. Vampires don't smell other vampire's very well when there is a heavy pall of smoke on the ground.

The End

Author Wendy Wilson

Born and raised in the suburbs of New York City, Wendy left the flatlands of Long Island for the mountains of Appalachia in the 80s. There she settled on a small farm and raised a variety of children, goats, sheep and pigs. She has worked in a library for most of her adult life and now, in retirement, has turned her love of reading books into a love of writing them. In December 2018 she won 2nd place in the online magazine Beneath the Rainbow's Christmas contest with the short story "Wishes Can Come True."

Made in the USA
San Bernardino, CA
23 November 2019